D0941340

I AM CANADA

BROTHERS IN ARMS

I AM CANADA

BROTHERS IN ARMS

The Siege of Louisbourg

by Don Aker

Scholastic Canada Ltd.

Toronto New York London Auckland Sydney
Mexico City New Delhi Hong Kong Buenos Aires

Copyright © 2015 by Don Aker. All rights reserved.

A Dear Canada Book. Published by Scholastic Canada Ltd.
SCHOLASTIC and I AM CANADA and logos are trademarks
and/or registered trademarks of Scholastic Inc.

www.scholastic.ca

Library and Archives Canada Cataloguing in Publication

Aker, Don, 1955-, author
Brothers in arms : the siege of Louisbourg / Don Aker.

(I am Canada)
Issued in print and electronic formats.
ISBN 978-1-4431-1959-7 (bound).—ISBN 978-1-4431-4675-3 (ebook).—
ISBN 978-1-4431-4676-0 (Apple edition)
1. Louisbourg (N.S.)—History—Siege, 1758—Juvenile fiction.
I. Title. II. Series: I am Canada

PS8551.K46B76 2015   jC813'.54   C2015-900443-8
                                               C2015-900444-6

No part of this publication may be reproduced or stored in a retrieval
system, or transmitted in any form or by any means, electronic,
mechanical, recording, or otherwise, without written permission of the
publisher, Scholastic Canada Ltd., 604 King Street West, Toronto, Ontario
M5V 1E1, Canada. In the case of photocopying or other reprographic
copying, a licence must be obtained from Access Copyright (Canadian
Copyright Licensing Agency), 1 Yonge Street, Suite 800, Toronto, Ontario
M5E 1E5 (1-800-893-5777).

6 5 4 3 2 1   Printed in Canada 114   15 16 17 18 19

The display type was set in AgfaRotisSerif.
The text was set in Minion.

First printing June 2015

For all of my teachers,
including every student who spent time
in my classroom

Prologue

The silence unnerves me.

After seven weeks of musket shots and cannon blasts, this ceasefire should be a godsend. After seven weeks of watching fellow soldiers and friends maimed and mutilated before my eyes, the stillness in the air should seem a blessing. But it is far from that. It is only the calm before the real storm. I understand this because I know the contents of the letter that Jean-Chrysostome Loppinot carries so solemnly beside me.

I should be proud that I, Sébastien de l'Espérance, am the soldier chosen from what remains of Louisbourg's garrison to accompany him as he delivers the letter to the British. But pride is not the emotion I feel. I carry the flag of my homeland high above my head. I march in the manner befitting a member of the Compagnies Franches de la Marine. But my heart is heavy.

Much of Louisbourg now lies in ruin. Many of the

1

buildings I once admired are merely smouldering rubble. There are breaches in the massive stone walls large enough for British infantry to enter en masse if they wish. The last of our great warships, Bienfaisant, *has been captured, and enemy vessels now fill the harbour. Governor de Boschenry, Chevalier de Drucour, had no option but to accept defeat. Continued resistance would have been suicide.*

But it is neither devastation nor defeat that weighs heaviest on my heart now. It is the single sentence written by Governor Drucour on the paper in Major Loppinot's hand.

The governor and his war council were horrified by the terms the British invaders have demanded. Although we were ultimately forced to surrender, we fought long and hard against overwhelming odds. We deserve to leave Louisbourg marching under our colours with muskets shouldered, a privilege befitting our bravery and our sacrifice. After all, our enemy received equal respect from my countrymen when the British garrison surrendered at Minorca only two years ago. Yet when Governor Drucour requested these honours of war, the British leaders flatly refused. In the briefest of notes, Major General Jeffery Amherst and Admiral Edward Boscawen wrote that they will agree to no conditions. Clearly, their wish is to humiliate us in our defeat.

In the face of such inflexibility, the war council had no choice. They unanimously agreed to refuse such indignity. In a single sentence, they have declared our willingness to die rather than suffer dishonour. It is this response that Major Loppinot and I must deliver.

I am not afraid to die. Having lived only eighteen years, there is much that I will never experience, but honour is everything. Without honour, what value has life?

But it is not only the lives of Louisbourg's remaining soldiers that will be lost after the British receive Drucour's response. The town sheltered within these walls has been home to nearly three thousand civilians who will also pay the price of British inflexibility.

But I am not thinking of those thousands now.

I am thinking of only one.

Chapter 1
June 1, 1758

"I've seen death masks that looked more joyous than you," said Guillaume as he walked beside me. The sounds of our boots against the cobblestones marked our progress along Louisbourg's Rue de l'Étang.

Guillaume Rousseau was well known among the Compagnies Franches de la Marine for his sense of humour, so I recognized his jibe as an attempt to lighten my mood. I forced a grin, but it no doubt bore closer resemblance to a scowl. "There can be no sterner man than Monsieur Desbarats in all of Île Royale," I said. "I fear he will refuse my request."

"But why should he?" asked Guillaume. "During our two years of service here in Louisbourg, you've proven yourself a valued soldier. Capitaine Boudier has agreed to vouch for you, has he not? And you aren't a penniless suitor, Sébastien. The money you've saved ensures that you can support a wife."

He spoke the truth, although many might have

doubted my financial means. After all, a private garrisoned at Louisbourg earned a fraction of what an ordinary labourer received. And some of that private's modest wages were earmarked for his uniform, his rations and other expenses. What remained was hardly enough to provide for a family. But Guillaume and I had been accustomed to hard work in our homeland and we had worked hard here, too, spending much of our off-duty time earning additional money repairing sections of the town's massive protective walls. While some wasted their extra earnings carousing in the town's taverns, Guillaume and I did not. Born to poor families in La Rochelle, France, where life had grown increasingly harsh as the threat of war with Britain loomed, we had learned to save every coin we could.

"Even as stern a man as Monsieur Desbarats will appreciate that you're no pauper," Guillaume continued.

I could see the soundness of his argument. But I had also seen the way Monsieur Desbarats glared at me each time I encountered his daughter in his shop.

Despite his dour, dismissive manner, I had spent the past two years working hard to prove myself worthy of Marie-Claire Desbarats, but I was glad Guillaume had agreed to accompany me as far as Monsieur Desbarats's door. I was fearless in my duties as a soldier, but I might have turned tail and run had Guillaume not been standing beside me.

I glanced at him for reassurance and he clapped a sturdy hand on my shoulder. I reached for the knocker, a round iron ring with the letter *D* at its centre, and drew a deep breath, then another. Guillaume gave me a nudge. I rapped the knocker twice.

In moments the door swung open and Monsieur Desbarats stood in the opening. "*Bonsoir*," he grunted. "What brings you to my door this evening?" His gruff voice and abrupt manner were well known, and the frown he wore suggested he was particularly aggravated by my presence before him.

I froze. My hesitation was, of course, ridiculous. As custom demanded, I had asked for and received his permission to court Marie-Claire, and our marriage was but a natural conclusion of that courtship. Yet I could not make my mouth form the words I had rehearsed for days. In fact, I could say nothing at all. My face burned like coals in an evening hearth.

"*Bonsoir*, Monsieur Desbarats," said Guillaume, taking charge of the awkward moment. "If it is convenient, sir, my good friend and brother in arms would like a moment of your time."

Monsieur Desbarats's gaze drifted from Guillaume to me. And then the impossible happened. He smiled.

*　　*　　*

Standing on the quay a short time later, I held Marie-Claire's hand in mine, her smooth palm soft against my calloused one. "Why did you not tell me your father could be so pleasant?" I asked.

She lowered her eyes and I recognized a conspiracy afoot. "He enjoys playing the ogre," she confessed. "He feels it benefits him in business. People are less likely to try to take advantage."

I smiled broadly. "Yet it is I who have taken advantage of him."

"How so?"

I brought her hand to my lips and kissed it. "I'm about to steal from his household the most beautiful woman in Île Royale."

She returned my smile with one that made my heart stumble and my mind whirl, and I had to force myself to think of the practical matters we now needed to address. After all, both our lives would change dramatically following our wedding. Before granting permission to marry his daughter, Monsieur Desbarats had insisted that I agree to leave the military as soon as my service was completed and assume a role in his business, a prospect I found daunting. But I would do anything for Marie-Claire. "Tomorrow I shall ask the priest to announce the banns of marriage during Mass," I said.

She nodded, her eyes shining. "Sébastien — " she began, but she was interrupted by someone shouting my name. We turned to see Guillaume running toward us, his boots flying over the cobblestones.

At first, I assumed he had learned of Monsieur Desbarats's response to my request and was hurrying to congratulate us. But as he drew nearer, I saw the expression on his face. Something was very wrong.

"The British!" he exclaimed when he reached us, his breathing ragged from his run. "Scores of their sails have been sighted — this time off Baie Gabarus. The British are preparing to come ashore!"

Chapter 2
June 2, 1758

Captain Boudier surveyed the soldiers of the Compagnies Franches de la Marine standing at attention. His eyes reflected approval at our readiness, which was to be expected. Each of the fifty men standing before him worked hard for that approval.

Louisbourg's garrison included more than three thousand soldiers, among them the Volontaires Étrangers, Artois and Bourgogne regiments as well as twenty-three other Compagnies Franches. My comrades and I were fortunate to be in the command of Captain Étienne Boudier. Soon after Guillaume and I arrived in Île Royale, we learned that, unlike Boudier, many of Louisbourg's commissioned officers were greedy and dishonest. And those vices were not the only ones shared by some of the officers. A few, such as Lieutenant Colonel Jean Mascle de Saint-Julhien, commander of the second battalion of the Artois and Bourgogne regiments, seemed incapable of providing strong leadership. Saint-Julhien's superior attitude offended everyone, even his fellow officers. While working on a section of the east wall one day, I'd overheard two of them talking. "Saint-Julhien!" one of them spat. "That man is incapable of desiring any good that does not originate with himself." Fortunately, Captain Boudier's only concern seemed to be Louisbourg's defence. He routinely pushed us to our very limits to ensure we were equal to the task, yet every man in his company respected him. We knew he valued our service. More important, we knew he would ask of us nothing he would not first demand of himself.

"*Compagnie*," he began, his face a grim mask in the early morning light, "the forces amassing against us are daunting."

No one in our company registered surprise. King George II had declared war on France weeks after Guillaume and I arrived in Île Royale. Since then the British had made no secret of their intent to capture our walled town, which in British eyes was a menace that needed to be eliminated. Their vessels had been sighted in increasing numbers off Île Royale's coast, and since early May a squadron of nine enemy ships had sailed back and forth across the entrance to our harbour, preventing French warships and cargo vessels from entering. Only the French privateers with their smaller vessels could outmaneuvre the lumbering square-riggers.

The blockade was of great concern to everyone because Louisbourg could not provide all the provisions that the colony needed to survive, relying as it did on supplies imported from many other places. With tensions rising in the face of those enemy ships, Governor Drucour had dispatched letters to the Minister of the Marine in France, outlining the growing threat and explaining Louisbourg's need for more ships and more troops. He had also sent a message to the Compagnies Franches officer Charles Deschamps de Boishébert, in Quebec, urging him to come to our aid. Boishébert was well known for his ability to assemble large numbers of irregular forces, among them native warriors who hated the British as much as we did.

We had all been hopeful that help would soon come. But now there was this news of the armada gathering at Baie Gabarus. Would aid arrive before the attack began?

"By our count," said Boudier, "the British ships outnumber ours eight to one."

Guillaume glanced at me. The astonishment on his face mirrored my own. Those numbers surely explained why our fourteen warships remained at anchor in the harbour.

"Gouverneur Drucour believes that retaliation by sea would be foolhardy," Boudier continued. "Our ships would first have to engage the squadron blockading us, and the sounds of their guns would alert the enemy at Baie Gabarus. More important, if our ships were disabled or captured, nothing would prevent the British from sailing unhindered into our harbour. Our fortifications are strong, but even they would not withstand unchecked bombardment from so many vessels."

A low muttering floated through the company as several of my comrades wondered aloud the question in my own mind — could we expect reinforcements?

Boudier began to speak again, and the muttering ceased. "Gouverneur Drucour has received word that five ships carrying six hundred eighty soldiers of the Cambis Regiment have arrived from France. With the British blockading the seaward approach, the ships have been forced to moor at a harbour a few days' march from here. The Cambis will complete their journey by land."

Several of my fellow soldiers voiced their relief while others thumped the backs of their comrades. In light of that armada at Baie Gabarus, this was welcome news.

"Are we to do nothing until the Cambis arrive?" murmured a soldier to my left. I turned to see Jacques Legrand's face lined with confusion, his expression making him appear even younger than usual. When the sixteen-year-old had arrived from France, Guillaume had wryly commented that the boy's family name seemed particularly unfitting. Legrand was a head shorter than most of his comrades, and many of us good-naturedly called him l'Enfant.

The boy had much to learn. Doing nothing would surely serve no purpose — something which Boudier made clear as he resumed his briefing. "The British know they cannot hope to defeat us by attacking from the sea. It is surely by land that they will make their approach."

He was right. Not only was the harbour entrance so narrow it could be easily defended, no other fortifications in North America were as imposing as Louisbourg's. More than a league of massive walls surrounded the town, the western wall as high as five men, and even wider across. Six pentagonal bastions located along these walls provided excellent vantage points from which artillerymen could fire their cannons. And Louisbourg's defences extended even beyond its walls. A small island in the harbour had a battery fortified with walls half as high as Louisbourg's itself; thirty-one guns stood at the ready there. Yes, my comrades could easily drive back a naval assault, which was why the British would surely approach by land. Louisbourg was overlooked by nearby hills. If the British were to mount an attack from that elevation, the outcome might not go in our favour. It was essential that our forces keep the enemy from making landfall.

And it was this mission that Boudier announced now. "Gouverneur Drucour has ordered reinforcements be sent to all possible landing sites to drive the enemy back. Several companies will march to Anse de la Cormorandière, Pointe Platte and Pointe Blanche," he said, referring to beaches west and southwest of us. "Others will head north to Anse à Gauthier. Our company will proceed to the seaward side of the town, where we will join armed civilians taking up positions. In the face of such a threat, every able-bodied man is needed." He scanned the company. "Any questions?"

There were none. Boudier nodded, then proceeded to give us our orders.

Moments later, our muskets shouldered, we marched through the town toward Bastion Maurepas and Bastion Brouillan, which overlooked the sea. The expressions on the faces of our

14

older, experienced comrades were grave, unlike those of us younger soldiers. Guillaume's ruddy face bore an especially wide grin. He was as eager as I to put our training to use against the British. After all, we had known this day would come. Since the Treaty of Aix-la-Chapelle had reverted ownership of Louisbourg to our motherland, its people had known it was only a matter of time before the British tried to reclaim the prize they had lost. But we were ready for them.

We had to be.

Chapter 3
June 4, 1758

The rising sun revealed lines on the faces of the soldiers standing guard with me in the Bastion Brouillan. The evening before, the distant sound of an explosion had drawn every man's eyes toward the west. Even now, many of my comrades continued to gaze in that direction.

"Surely that was more than cannon fire, Sébastien," Guillaume said. For nearly two days now, we had listened to the periodic discharge of heavy guns in the distance, but none had been as thunderous as the one the previous evening.

I shrugged, staring out at the waves that broke against the rocks beyond. The ocean had been rough for days, yet the sound of that explosion had carried clearly above the unending roll and crash of the sea. I was at a loss to explain it. Fortunately, I did not have to.

"Compagnie!"

Corporal Pierre Grimaud came striding toward us along the massive wall. We lurched to attention, awaiting whatever news he might have for us.

"Our orders have changed," he said when he reached us. "*Suivez-moi.*"

Shouldering our muskets, we followed him as he led us toward the Porte Maurepas, where the rest of our comrades had already assembled before Captain Boudier.

"*Compagnie,*" Boudier began. "I expect you heard the explosion last evening."

Nods and murmurs from my comrades confirmed this.

"Yesterday, British guns began bombarding our comrades at Anse de la Cormorandière. One of them struck a supply of our gunpowder and there were casualties."

I shook my head at this news, as did Guillaume. But we had no time to worry about which soldiers had been injured. Or killed.

"Gouverneur Drucour has ordered reinforcements and additional cannons be sent to the area," explained Boudier. "Prepare to leave for Anse de la Cormorandière within the quarter hour."

My thoughts turned to Marie-Claire. I longed to see her before the company's march to the cove, longed to hold her in my arms and tell her *au revoir*, but I knew this was not possible. We had to move quickly if we were to keep the enemy at bay.

*   *   *

A handful of British masts poked through the thick fog along the shoreline. Guillaume spotted them, too, and turned to grin at me. This was surely the moment we had trained for.

Ahead of us, Captain Boudier raised his arm and all fifty men halted. He began barking commands, and we immediately broke formation and poured over the ridge, past the cannons and swivel guns. The trees that had once grown here had been felled and rolled to the water's edge, their trunks and tangled roots and branches blocking access to the cove's two main beaches. With little natural protection on the hillside that sloped toward the water, we set to work carving shallow trenches to give us cover.

Moments later, Guillaume elbowed me. "Sébastien! Do you see?"

I looked to where he was pointing — a gaping hole far to our right. It was all that remained after British gunners had blown up that supply of gunpowder. At least the fog and high surf during the last few days had kept the British from attempting a landing, but we all knew this reprieve would not last.

"Hopefully," I said, nodding toward the damage, "that strike was British luck, not skill."

Guillaume nodded. "Those redcoats will quiver

in their boots when they see Guillaume Rousseau firing at them."

I grinned at his confidence, and we set to work on our trenches again.

As we dug, Boudier moved across the hillside, stopping momentarily to speak to my comrades. From time to time, the wind brought snatches of his comments to my ears, some of them offering advice, many of them encouragement. Finally he reached Guillaume and me. Surveying our work, he nodded approvingly. "This weather will break soon," he warned. "When it does, the British will be upon us. We cannot allow them to make land-fall here."

An hour later, having finished our trench, Guillaume and I lowered ourselves into position to await the assault. I lay there, my eyes trained on the water's edge, because I could see no farther. The fog had continued to thicken, masking even the waves that crashed against the shore.

My musket gripped in my hands, my thoughts turned again to Marie-Claire. Yes, I would soon be fighting to defend French rule in the New World, but I would also be fighting for the woman I loved. The woman who, God willing, would soon be my wife.

Chapter 4
June 8, 1758

Boudier was wrong about one thing. Four days had passed, yet the British still had not attempted a landing. While the weather had improved somewhat, fog continued to shroud the coast as the surf pounded relentlessly against the shore. Lying now in the pre-dawn darkness of our trench, I could hear enormous waves shatter on the rocky beach, and I began to wonder whether the British might abandon their plans to attack.

Three days earlier, Governor Drucour himself had ridden to Anse de la Cormorandière to tell our leaders that half of the Cambis Regiment was waiting for small boats to take them to Baie des Espagnols, where they would begin their march to the town. Captain Boudier's voice betrayed his frustration when he shared this information with us, but he encouraged all of us to remain strong and prepared.

We were grateful to learn yesterday that the first contingent of the Cambis troops had marched into Louisbourg, followed by thirty Micmac warriors. My comrades cheered the news. It was exactly what we needed after days of lying cold and cramped in our trenches. Beside me now, Guillaume snored. We took turns keeping watch, and I chose to remain awake in the hour before dawn. During the night I had sensed a change in the air. The crash of the waves told me that the surf still ran high, but the dampness of the past three days had lessened, suggesting that the fog might at last begin to lift. I kept my face turned to the east, my eyes watching for the first rays of light to confirm what I suspected.

"Guillaume!" I hissed minutes later.

He jolted awake. "*Oui*, Sébastien?"

I pointed toward the water. The fog had pulled away from the shore, exposing the dark silhouettes of enemy ships on the sea. Beside them, smaller shapes bobbed on the water, flat-bottomed long-boats already filled with enemy soldiers, some packed so tightly the men were forced to stand. Astonishingly, the British had launched them under cover of darkness without making a sound. One group now made its way in the direction of Pointe Platte, another headed toward Pointe Blanche, while a third flotilla rowed toward us.

Sounds of muskets being readied in the trenches

on either side told us our comrades had arrived at the same realization. The invasion had begun.

Guillaume clapped a hand on my shoulder. "At last," he breathed.

I shared his excitement. For the very first time, we would not be using our muskets in practice or for hunting. We would be firing our weapons as soldiers in defence of our king and our country.

And Marie-Claire.

Explosions ripped through the calm as cannons aboard the closest ships now began to fire. Water sprayed in all directions as cannonballs fell short of us and struck its churning surface. But it would not be long before the British artillerymen found their range. I raised my musket, aiming it toward the boats already approaching the shore.

"*Compagnie!*" shouted Boudier, and every man under his command turned toward the captain. "I have an order from Lieutenant Colonel Mascle de Saint-Julhien."

Beside me, Guillaume swore under his breath. Our first day here, a few of us had failed to suppress groans at learning that Saint-Julhien was in command, yet Captain Boudier had been quick to show his annoyance at our response. We would not make that mistake again.

"You are to withhold fire until the boats are

within close range," called Boudier. "No one is to shoot until given the order."

I scanned the British longboats. While most of our attackers wore the red coats I expected to see, others wore a variety of uniforms, among them bold Highland tartans. All of the men not busy rowing clung fast to the gunwales as the boats bobbed like corks in the high waves.

Artillery fire from the ships continued to punch the air. I suppressed a shudder at each explosion. Yet still we waited, our weapons trained on the approaching flotilla. A huge wave capsized two of the boats, men and muskets suddenly disappearing from sight. Within moments a few heads broke the surface as men flailed in the pounding surf. Only two of the invaders managed to reach an overturned boat before their sodden uniforms pulled them under.

I looked at Guillaume, his eyes reflecting the same dismay that was washing over me now. Despite wanting to rout the British, neither of us was eager to watch men drown. To be killed in battle was one thing, but to die from waves instead of wounds seemed a mockery.

A third boat capsized and more British soldiers vanished beneath the waves. But the remaining boats kept closing the distance between them and the shoreline, making me wonder if we would ever hear the order to fire. Finally, just as the keels of the first boats dragged on the bottom, it came. *"Feu!"*

The cove erupted with gunfire as our muskets, cannons and swivel guns bombarded the enemy. Musket shot tore through red coats suddenly darkened with blood, their wearers spun like tops or thrown backwards into the waves. Fragments of boats shattered by artillery fire flew in all directions, piercing men like jagged spears. Most horrifying of all was the sight of a man cut in half by a cannonball that tore through his body and then through the boat he and his comrades were struggling to beach.

Riddled with holes, other boats quickly filled with water and sank. Soldiers' cries were lost amid the crash of the surf and the roar of gunfire. This was more slaughter than skirmish, more like shooting pigs in a pen than defending a stretch of beach.

My ears ringing from weapon fire and my eyes smarting from the flare of gunpowder, I concentrated on loading, shooting and reloading, trying to make every shot count despite the revulsion I felt each time musket shot smashed through flesh and bone. Beside me Guillaume was doing the same, focusing on driving the enemy back, keeping the British from gaining the foothold they desired. *"Mon Dieu!"* he muttered, shaking his head as he reloaded.

By now, many of the boats remaining on the water were retreating, but the heavy surf, much of it crimson with blood, was still taking its toll. Through the smoke-filled air, Guillaume and I watched, mystified, as one boat, its sides now looking more like cheesecloth than wood, somehow managed to remain afloat. A gust of wind blew some of the smoke aside. The occupants of the boat, brawny Highlanders, had stuffed the holes with the thick wool of their tartans. I wondered if they would as easily be able to stop the blood flowing from their wounds.

The barrage continued for fifteen minutes until, above the tumult, drums signalled the companies to cease firing.

Guillaume grasped my shoulder. *"Nous sommes vainqueurs!"* he shouted.

But after what I had just seen, I was less certain of our victory. While others cheered our success, I rose and made my way toward Captain Boudier.

Guillaume followed. "Is there something wrong, Sébastien?" he asked.

"Je ne sais pas."

When I reached Boudier and Saint-Julhien, I saluted them both. *"Capitaine,"* I said, "I request permission to scout the area to the east."

"For what reason?" asked Boudier.

I told him of three boats I had watched among the others that had retreated. "They disappeared while rounding that outcropping," I explained, pointing to where I had last seen them. "They never reappeared, so they may have beached on the other side with the intent to attack us from behind. Higher ground would give them the advantage."

"No one could scale the cliffs on either side of this cove," Saint-Julhien scoffed, "and certainly not with weapons in hand. If the soldiers you saw in those boats survived," he continued, "they are surely trapped on the spit of land beneath those cliffs."

Boudier seemed less certain of that fact. Turning to Saint-Julhien, he said, "I respectfully ask your permission, as a precautionary measure, to send these two men to scout the area."

"As you wish," Saint-Julhien muttered, already moving off to survey the damage the British guns had wrought.

Boudier turned to us. "Report what you learn directly to me," he said.

* * *

"You think I am being too cautious," I said to Guillaume as we crept toward the bluff above Anse de la Cormorandière. It was the first either of us had spoken since leaving the shore below. Now and then the breeze brought faint cheers from our comrades.

Guillaume turned a grave face toward me. His eyes held a haunted look. *"Non,"* he replied. "It is better that we check."

I nodded, now understanding the reason for his silence. My own mind still reeled from the gore we had witnessed earlier, and I suspected Guillaume was struggling with those same gruesome images.

We continued in silence through the bushes and tall grass, the only vegetation that remained, since the forest had fallen to French axes. At last we reached the outcropping. Dropping to the ground, we crawled toward its edge, peering through the grass that screened us. Far below on a fingernail of beach were the three boats. They had been joined by two others, and more than eighty British soldiers had begun to make their way up the cliff toward us, their muskets strapped to their backs. Although the pounding of the surf masked their voices, I could well imagine their satisfaction at having made landfall after so disastrous an attempt in the cove. And their slow but determined progress up the rock face suggested that nothing would keep them from scaling it. Except Guillaume and me.

I slipped my musket off my shoulder, but a hand gripped my arm. *"Non!"* hissed Guillaume.

"But we *must*," I breathed.

"Against such numbers?" He shook his head. "We lack enough shot to keep all of them from reaching the summit. And what if more boats arrive?"

Peering again at the enemy climbing toward us, I was overwhelmed by the sight of these British invaders advancing on French soil. My mind filled with images of Marie-Claire, and I wanted nothing more than to take aim at the nearest redcoat. But Guillaume was right. We needed to warn our comrades.

* * *

"Capitaine!" we shouted in unison as we ran down the slope toward Boudier, who was inspecting a cannon.

Boudier's face darkened as we approached.

"The British are ashore!" called Guillaume.

"How many?" he demanded.

"Quatre-vingts," I gasped. "Maybe more."

"Come with me!" he ordered.

We followed him across the hillside toward Saint-Julhien, who stood looking toward the sea, his hands clasped behind his back. Hearing footsteps hurrying toward him, he turned. The self-satisfied smile on his lips vanished.

"Sir!" said Boudier when we reached him. "My men have something to report."

"*Oui?*" he snapped.

As quickly as we could, we told him about the boats that had beached beneath the bluff, and our fear that others would soon join them.

He raised his eyes heavenward and sighed. "They may have reached the shore, but their landing affords them no advantage. The British cannot possibly scale that cliff with weapons in hand."

"But, sir," said Guillaume, "they are doing that very thing. Sébastien and I saw them."

"I am sure you saw them *try*," he said, "but did any reach the summit?"

"*Non,*" Guillaume muttered.

"We didn't stay to watch them succeed," I said. "We thought it better to report the news to you at once."

Saint-Julhien nodded toward the surf and I reluctantly followed his gaze. Shattered bodies continued to roll in waves that still ran red, and I swallowed sudden nausea. I focused my attention once more on Saint-Julhien as he spoke again. "We have driven the British back. Any efforts to outflank us from that beach will be useless."

"Sir," said Boudier, clipping each word. "With your permission, I would like to reposition my company on our left flank as a defensive measure."

Saint-Julhien waved a hand as though brushing aside a fly, then seemed to notice the intensity in Boudier's words. He nodded curtly.

Saluting him, Boudier turned and strode past us, Guillaume and I falling into step behind. Once more, I was proud to be in his command.

After quickly sharing with our comrades the news of our discovery, Boudier barked orders that each of us followed to the letter. Within moments everyone in our company had taken up new positions above the cove, prepared to repel any enemy soldiers who might attack our left flank.

Lying in wait, I should have felt heartened that our vastly outnumbered garrison had been able to turn back the enemy with so few casualties. But I was not. The only thought in my head was the sight of those British soldiers making their way up the rock face.

*   *   *

"Do you see him?" Guillaume whispered beside me. His words were barely audible above the musket fire that repeatedly cracked the air.

"*Oui*," I replied, my eyes following the figure moving furtively through the bushes ahead of us.

If not for his bright red coat, I might have missed him, so I was once more grateful to the British for their choice of uniform. The dark blue livery that my comrades and I wore was much more difficult to detect.

Kneeling, I drew a cartridge from my belt and bit off the paper end to expose the black powder. My movements were mere reflexes, routines drilled into us again and again to prepare our muskets for firing — half-cock the hammer, pour gunpowder into the priming pan, close the frizzen, place the butt of the musket against my left calf, pour more powder down the muzzle, insert the cartridge, plunge the ramrod into the barrel, tamp down the lead ball and powder. The whole process took scant moments, as instinctive to me as breathing. And why not? I had been doing it without interruption since the enemy had appeared on our left flank.

I raised my musket and sighted down the barrel at the soldier, anticipating his next movement. I waited, holding my breath, and then squeezed the trigger. The sharp report of my musket joined others around me as the redcoat fell back, a lead ball now deep in his chest.

The British soldiers had scaled the cliff before we could stop them, a feat that seemed to have made them even bolder than they had appeared that morning. And others had clearly joined those we'd seen on the beach beyond the outcropping. Eager to rout us, they had made their way stealthily yet swiftly toward our position. Had we not been expecting them, we might well have been overpowered because, as I had feared, their position on higher ground gave them the advantage. As it was, several of our comrades had been wounded and at least two were feared dead. But the enemy, too, had suffered casualties, which had kept them from advancing farther. And we'd received word that Saint-Julhien had ordered the Artois and Bourgogne soldiers to reinforce our numbers, so we were confident we could hold the enemy back. After all, what could a few boatloads of British accomplish in the face of a thousand French soldiers and Micmac warriors?

"De l'Espérance! Rousseau!"

Corporal Grimaud crept toward us as a shot whistled through the air, clipping his tricorne and knocking it from his head. Beside me, Guillaume's musket rang out, its target the soldier who had fired at the corporal. A cry of pain confirmed that Guillaume's shot had found its mark.

"*Oui?*" I responded, hoping Grimaud was bringing word of reinforcements.

"Fall back."

I blinked at him. *"Excusez-moi?"*

"We are retreating."

I could not believe my ears. "Retreating?"

"Are we not keeping them from advancing?" Guillaume demanded, as surprised as I. "Surely with reinforcements — "

Grimaud shook his head. "Saint-Julhien has changed his mind. He fears that more British soldiers may come ashore and block the road to Louisbourg. If that happens — "

Another shot rang out, cutting off his words, but we didn't need to hear them. We understood the threat. If the British blocked the road and kept our troops at Anse de la Cormorandière from reaching Louisbourg, the town's garrison would be drastically reduced in number.

I had not served for two years without learning to obey orders, but I was mystified by Saint-Julhien's thinking. "Our numbers here at the moment are far greater," I said, amid the burst of more musket fire. "If Saint-Julhien would only send the men he promised — "

"He's made his decision," interrupted Grimaud, although something in his voice suggested he, too, questioned Saint-Julhien's plan of action. "You will return to the town immediately. Is that clear?"

"Oui, caporal," Guillaume and I replied, then

watched Grimaud move off to inform the other members of our company of their new orders.

Moments later as we made our way along the void, skirting enemy fire, I could not help but wonder if Saint-Julhien would come to regret his decision. Yes, it was imperative that the town be fully garrisoned. But had Governor Drucour not stressed the importance of keeping the British from establishing a foothold at Anse de la Cormorandière? Despite the strength of Louisbourg's fortifications and weaponry, could the garrison repel an assault by land?

More musket fire interrupted my thoughts, and the ground to my left exploded as lead shot punched into it. Ducking our heads, Guillaume and I followed our comrades toward the safety of Louisbourg's walls.

* * *

Companies that had reached Louisbourg before us had clearly raised the alarm in advance of our arrival. As we approached, the British at our backs, French weapons fired over our heads at the enemy, covering our advance toward the Porte de la Reine on the southwest side. Smoke and the repeated boom of cannons filled the salt air as we made our way forward, many of us helping comrades limping from their wounds.

Between us, Guillaume and I supported the

bloody figure of young Jacques Legrand, who had been shot in the belly and now groaned with each step he took. Both Guillaume and I had eluded enemy fire and could have reached the gate sooner, but we would not leave behind an injured comrade. Sadly, we could do nothing for those who had been captured or now lay dead.

Behind us, Captain Boudier continued to shout encouragement. As we all knew, he would be the last of our company to enter the gate.

"I — I can go no farther," wheezed Legrand, his breathing ragged and wet.

"*Oui*, Jacques, you *can*," I said as I grasped his arm slung over my shoulder. Guillaume and I were all but carrying him now. "We're nearly there." I spoke the truth. We were within a hundred paces of the gate and the cannon fire above our heads was keeping British weapons from finding their mark. The enemy force that had been at our heels earlier was now too distant to be a threat.

"*Non*," Legrand gasped, "I cannot." He released a groan that seemed to begin in his toes, and his legs suddenly folded beneath him.

Still supporting our comrade with one arm, Guillaume handed me his musket with the other, then lifted Jacques clear of the ground. Cradling him, he continued forward as I followed, giving silent thanks for the cannons that continued to boom overhead.

It would be much later, however, when we would learn that this defensive action, which had saved our lives, had also sealed our fate.

Chapter 5
June 10, 1758

The rain slapping the barracks windows in watery sheets made it seem as though the Atlantic Ocean had breached its shores and now surged against the garrison walls. Although my comrades and I knew we would be soaked the moment we stepped outside, none of us cursed the miserable weather. The British would not be mounting an assault if they were unable to keep their powder dry.

"Legrand is still very weak," said Boudier, who had once again been to the hospital to check on the wounded before addressing the company, "but he remains alive. He lost a great deal of blood, but the surgeon-major believes his youth is in his favour. He may yet survive his wound. We can only wait. And pray," he added.

I knew the entire company must share my relief. We had been awaiting news of our wounded comrades, especially l'Enfant, and the faces of every man standing with me now mirrored my own. Having seen two of our fellow soldiers cut down at Anse de la Cormorandière, and three more killed

during our retreat, we were grateful that one life
— especially that of a person so young — might
yet be spared.

Christophe Gilbert and Édouard Villeneuve,
senior soldiers in our company, seemed especially
thankful to learn of Legrand's condition. They
had taken the boy under their wing upon learning
that he had come from Lyon, where they too had
been born. The concern on their faces was now
tempered with relief.

Despite this good news, Boudier's expression
remained grim. Reports from the various regiments indicated that 114 French soldiers had been
lost on June 8, most either injured or captured,
but many of them killed. It was the deaths that
were especially grievous, and not just because lives
had been lost. Those soldiers had died in vain. The
garrison had failed in its most important mission
— to keep the British from making landfall.

Our leaders were clearly stunned by this failure, having watched the victory of that early
morning snatched from their hands. During the
hours that followed, there had been much talk
about where the blame for this failure lay. As my
comrades and I carried out new orders following
our return, we listened to officers mutter among
themselves. Many criticized Saint-Julhien for not

having posted a lookout above the cove in advance of the assault, a measure that would have kept us from being caught unawares. Others faulted him for giving a premature order to fire upon the longboats. They believed that, had he waited longer, our guns could have wiped out the entire landing force. Still others blamed him for ordering the retreat so soon. "No more than one hundred fifty British were able to beach in that first wave," grumbled one officer. "If our thousand soldiers at Anse de la Cormorandière had been given the opportunity, they could have turned the redcoats back easily."

I silently agreed. However, as the afternoon wore on, we learned that Saint-Julhien was not the only leader to make mistakes. When the French commanders at Pointe Platte and Pointe Blanche heard what was happening at Anse de la Cormorandière, they, too, had ordered their men back to the town. However, only the commander at Pointe Blanche had ensured that the arms at his location — with the exception of the cannons — were destroyed beforehand. In ordering a hastier retreat, the commander at Pointe Platte had left behind swivel guns, cannons and stores of ammunition that the British could now use against us — further arming an enemy that already outnumbered us.

To counteract their error in judgment, Governor Drucour had sent fifty soldiers of the Volontaires Étrangers regiment to destroy the twenty-four-pounder left behind at Pointe Blanche. But they had turned back when they discovered the British already occupied that position. Drucour then took steps to increase the garrison, ordering the men at two locations outside the town to abandon those posts and regroup within its walls. Now that the British had breached the shores of Île Royale, Drucour reasoned it would be only a matter of days before they attacked those positions from the rear, and he had no desire to lose more soldiers. He was confident that the island battery and the one at Pointe à Rochefort, along with our warships, would still be able to keep enemy ships from entering the harbour.

The garrison was also increased by the arrival of the other half of the Cambis Regiment, who had marched into Louisbourg shortly after our retreat. This good news, however, did not make it easier for our company to carry out the orders we had received that afternoon. Several buildings stood outside the wall, many of them houses, and Drucour feared that those buildings would soon provide cover for enemy soldiers. He ordered them all destroyed, and Guillaume and I were among the men given that duty.

Guillaume was as disheartened as I by our task. As he put a torch to the first building, he winced as if the flames licking over the boards were scorching him, too. I winced as well. After all, we had spent much of the past two years in Louisbourg working as builders — the limestone in this part of Île Royale contained sandstone, which weakened the mortar in the stone walls and required frequent repairs. Yet we had been tasked with destroying what others had so carefully constructed. Even now as we stood before Captain Boudier two days later, smoke from those smouldering piles of wet rubble still hung heavy in the air.

Having shared his news about Legrand, Boudier let his gaze slide over the company before speaking again. "No one can know what the future holds, but we are soldiers who serve at the pleasure of King Louis. Our sole duty is to keep Louisbourg from falling into British hands. You fought well at Anse de la Cormorandière, and I know you will continue to do so in the days ahead. When you resume your positions at the bastions today, remember your fallen brothers. Their sacrifice will give you strength."

He hesitated and an odd expression rippled across his face, making me wonder if he had more to say. But then he simply nodded and strode off.

No sooner had I stepped outside the barracks than I was drenched by driving rain. Grimacing, I tugged down my tricorne to keep the torrent from my eyes. Guillaume did the same. As we made our way toward the Bastion Brouillan, he asked, "Do you think the captain had more to tell us?"

"*Oui*," I replied, wondering how he knew I had been mulling that very thing. Apparently, our bond as friends and brothers in arms had grown even stronger since the British had appeared off our shores. "Do you suppose it was something more about our comrades in hospital?"

Guillaume shrugged.

"I th-th-think I kn-know," said a voice behind us.

It had to be Renard Gaston. Having stuttered since he was a child, he seldom spoke, and in the two years I had known him, he had never once begun a conversation. I was astonished to hear him speak now.

"What do you know, Renard?" I asked as he came abreast of us.

Beneath his sopping tricorne, Renard's face flushed. He spoke haltingly, every word clearly a challenge. But by the time we reached the Bastion Brouillan, he'd shared with us what he had learned the previous night.

Renard had been assigned guard duty just

outside the governor's apartments, where the war council discussed Louisbourg's plight, planning our defence. While at his post, he had overheard voices raised behind the closed door, and it was clear that tempers were high. A short time later, two senior officers had come out, shaking their heads and muttering about what had unfolded inside.

Because Renard most often communicated with hand gestures and facial expressions, some of the officers mistakenly assumed he was deaf. As a result, many spoke loosely around him, wrongly believing him incapable of overhearing what they said. Those two officers had spoken heatedly to each other about Drucour's decision regarding three of the warships at anchor in the harbour.

Renard told us that, following our retreat the previous day, our naval commanders had sent Drucour a letter requesting his permission to sail out of the harbour after dark. Believing that Louisbourg was now doomed, they wanted to ensure the safety of their ships and sailors so they might fight for King Louis another day. The members of the war council rejected the idea of naval officers abandoning Louisbourg's soldiers and civilians, but Drucour had agreed to allow three of the warships, *Comète*, *Bizarre* and *Echo,* to leave.

Upon hearing Renard's account, Guillaume and I immediately turned toward the harbour. It was true. Those three ships were gone.

"Can it be?" asked Guillaume, dumbfounded. "Are we truly doomed?"

I thought of the odd expression I had seen on Captain Boudier's face. Was it anger at those naval officers for having abandoned the colony? Or was it despair because he, too, felt our situation was now hopeless?

I shrugged. "Didn't Boudier tell us that no one can know what the future holds?" I asked. "And did he not remind us that our sole duty is to keep Louisbourg from falling into British hands? That's the only truth we need concern ourselves with now."

Nodding, Guillaume gripped my shoulder. "You're right, my friend." And then he grinned. "Those redcoats will quiver in their boots — "

" — when they see Guillaume Rousseau firing at them," I finished for him, grinning in return.

But the smile on my face was merely a mask, the routine response of a friend and brother in arms. In my heart I felt none of that certainty. I had only to imagine those three ships hauling anchor and slipping away in the dead of night to accept what I believed Boudier already knew. We *were* doomed. But I also knew that this did not change what was required of me. I would do everything in my power to halt the British invasion. If need be, I would lay down my life in defence of the town because the lives of the civilians who had made their home in Louisbourg depended on me.

Marie-Claire depended on me.

I had often heard people say there is no such thing as love at first sight, but I would argue they had never laid eyes on Marie-Claire Desbarats. More than two years ago, Guillaume and I had arrived at Louisbourg after a very difficult winter crossing aboard the ship *Rhinocéros*. I should have been grateful to see land on that cold March day, but I continued to suffer from crushing home-sickness. I missed my family more than I thought possible, and I wanted nothing more than to return to France, despite there being no future for me there. The best opportunity available to commoners like Guillaume and me was in the service of King Louis XV in this untamed land, but still I longed for home. That is, until my eyes fell on the beautiful girl standing on the quay watching *Rhinocéros* navigate the ice in the harbour. By the time Guillaume and I disembarked, she had vanished. It would be days before I saw her again, this time with her family in the garrison church. And it would take me several weeks more to muster the courage to speak to her.

Guillaume tormented me mercilessly the few times my path crossed hers and I was unable to do more than stand dumbstruck. It was, in fact, she who eventually spoke first. Guillaume and I had entered a shop one spring day in search of a hunting knife and found her there assisting the owner, who we later learned was her father. When she greeted us I could do little more than stammer. Fortunately, Guillaume's good humour and easy manner helped lessen my nervousness, and I was eventually able to make conversation with her. That was our beginning.

Looking now at the void where those three warships had once anchored, I could not help but fear that the British invasion heralded our ending.

Chapter 6
June 11, 1758

"But how could Capitaine Boudier order you to do something so *dangerous*?" Marie-Claire demanded, her face creased with worry.

In the ten days since I had asked her father for her hand in marriage, I had been given leave to see her only twice. And because of the growing threat of the British, I'd been able to spend only moments with her each time. I had no desire to upset her this evening, yet that's exactly what I had done when I told her the task I was to undertake. I cleared my throat. "Capitaine Boudier didn't order us to do this," I replied. "Guillaume and I volunteered."

"But *why*?" Sitting beside me in her father's parlour, she reached for my hands, her fingers entwining my own as though trying to hold me to that spot.

I suddenly felt like Renard Gaston as I struggled to voice my thoughts. Since our retreat on June 8, the entire garrison had been functioning in thirds: one-third at the ready, one-third in their rooms fully clothed and prepared for action at a moment's notice, and one-third allowed to sleep. I was fortunate that Boudier had granted me permission to see Marie-Claire before my departure, and I had no wish to waste our precious time together quarrelling. "You know the British are pressing their attack on the town by land," I told her, trying to keep my voice even. I had no wish to alarm her more than she already was. "If we're to be prepared for it, there is much that our leaders need to know. The exact numbers of the enemy's forces, how they're planning their approach, when they seek to — "

"But surely there are scouts who can provide this information," she interrupted, a pleading note in her voice.

I nodded. "Yes, but the sheer size of the British force makes it likely that — " I paused, silently cursing my tactlessness. I let my thought hang in the air.

Marie-Claire was not fooled. "It makes it likely," she began, her voice little more than a whisper, "that some scouts will be captured or . . . " She looked away, her hands gripping mine even tighter.

"Nothing will stop me from returning to you," I said softly. "I promise."

"But why must *you* do this?" she asked, her eyes glistening.

I had no need to remind her that Guillaume and I knew the area as well as anyone. Besides rebuilding the town's crumbling walls to supplement our modest income, we had hunted for game throughout the surrounding countryside to use as barter for the things we needed. In fact, the circumstance that had brought me to her father's shop the day we met was to replace the hunting knife I had broken while cleaning the carcass of a stag.

What I needed her to understand was that I could do nothing less than use that knowledge in Louisbourg's defence because it would be in *her* defence as well. When I learned about those three ships abandoning our town, I suddenly realized that I must do more than wait for the enemy to come to us. Some of our leaders might have accepted that Louisbourg was doomed, but I could not. I *would* not. When my sentry duty had ended the previous day, I'd gone to Boudier with my offer to scout the area and bring back information about British troops and their movements. And when Guillaume later learned what I had done, he immediately did the same. I tried to change his mind, but he shrugged and reminded me that he knew the area as well as I.

He said nothing more, did not try to explain what I already knew — that he was my brother in arms and, where I went, he would follow. Some things did not have to be put into words.

Sitting beside Marie-Claire now, I longed to have her understand that nothing was more important to me than the life the two of us planned to build together. I had no desire to put myself in harm's way. But if doing so might ensure that we would get to live that life together, I could do nothing else.

As the thin grey light of early morning began to seep into the parlour, I knew no words would truly serve my purpose. All I could do was squeeze her hands and repeat my promise: "Nothing will stop me from returning to you."

And I silently prayed that it was a promise I would be able to keep.

*   *   *

I found Guillaume waiting for me at the gate, studying the black marble plaque mounted on the inside, its gilded letters spelling *Porte Dauphine*. Of course, the letters held no meaning for him. Guillaume had never learned to read. What attracted him to the plaque was its crafts-manship, which he once told me reminded him of the work of his father, who was a carver.

Hearing my footsteps, he turned to greet me. "Was she very upset?" he asked.

I nodded. "She wanted me to assure you that you, too, will be in her prayers."

"Ah, it's those redcoats who are in need of her prayers," he jested. But he knew as well as I how dangerous our mission would be.

"De l'Espérance! Rousseau!"

Captain Boudier strode in our direction. As he reached us, he extended his hands, a fresh leather cartridge box in each. "This cursed damp weather plays havoc with gunpowder," he said. "It will not hurt to have additional ammunition."

Guillaume and I took the cartridge boxes from him, attaching them to our waist belts. Boudier knew we always took great pains to keep our cartridges dry, so the reason he had come to the Porte Dauphine surely had little to do with ammunition.

He cleared his throat. "You will be careful, *oui*?"

"*Oui, capitaine*," we chorused.

"*Bonne chance*," he said, saluting us before nodding at the guards, who raised the bar and swung the gate wide.

Leaving the town's walls behind us, Guillaume and I passed the remains of the first buildings we had razed. The hard rain of the day before had lessened to a steady drizzle, but a few tendrils of smoke still rose from the scorched timbers.

Guillaume and I walked in silence. We thought it safer not to travel the route the company had taken to Anse de la Cormorandière. Instead we threaded our way across terrain dotted with stumps of trees that had been felled for construction and to provide unobstructed views from the town. Our feet scarcely made a sound as we moved forward.

I thought of the last time we had ventured beyond the walls before the British arrived. We had been tracking a stag with hoofprints the size of small platters, and we finally came upon it feeding near a stream. Guillaume halted and was raising his musket to fire when a large brown snake emerged from the undergrowth and slithered across his boot. As brave a man as I knew Guillaume to be, he had a morbid fear of snakes, and he leaped back, shouting and startling the stag. With a flick of its tail, it bounded away before we could even raise our muskets. I began to chuckle, as much at Guillaume's embarrassment as the distance he had leaped, which was considerable, and before long he was laughing, too. I longed to have reason to do the same now, but laughter was a part of our lives no longer. Death lurked everywhere.

Boudier had suggested that we focus our attention on Pointe Platte. Since our leaders already knew that Pointe Blanche was occupied by the British, they were interested in other areas along the coast where our enemy might be established, so we travelled in a southwest direction toward that stretch of shore.

As we continued, I thought of other members of our company who would also find themselves beyond the walls of the town that day. Some had previously been assigned to fill bags with dirt that would be used to strengthen the casemates within the walls of the Bastion du Roi. Because an attack was now a certainty, Governor Drucour wanted to provide shelter for women and children during the coming bombardment. The stone vaults would be as safe as anything *could* be in the face of British mortars. As I walked, I thought of my comrades shovelling wet earth yesterday, and in my imagination I saw myself turning the soil on my own land, Marie-Claire watching me from the doorway of our snug Île Royale home. As my mind played with that image, it added two small children, a boy and a girl, their colouring that of their mother. They played at her side, and Marie-Claire laughed at their antics as they —

"Did you hear that?" Guillaume hissed. He had

frozen in mid-step, his left arm raised in warning.

I silently chided myself. Inattention could cost a soldier his life. "I heard nothing," I whispered after a moment. "What did it sound like?"

"A voice," he replied softly. "Someone speaking at a distance." He listened a moment longer, then shook his head. "Perhaps I imagined it."

"Perhaps," I allowed. "It may have been the wind. It sometimes seems to moan."

He shrugged. *"Excusez-moi.* My nerves are as taut as bowstrings."

I waved his apology away. It was better that his senses were overly keen than for mine to wander as they had. Drawing a deep breath, I resumed my pace, this time focusing on every movement and sound around us.

* * *

"Mon Dieu!" Guillaume breathed.

We had been walking for nearly two hours, stopping frequently to listen for signs of the enemy. Twice we'd been forced to take cover in the long grass as British soldiers scoured the area, clearly performing their own reconnaissance. But we had reached our destination undetected, and we now peered over a rise just above the expanse of Pointe Platte.

The sight before us was astonishing. Beside us,

a brook spilled down the slope and meandered toward the ocean, and the enemy had established camps on either side of it. This was no surprise, since the brook was a source of drinking water. What amazed Guillaume and me was the sea of tents pitched before us. Thousands of soldiers were encamped there.

But it was not just the sheer number of men that astounded us. It was the preparations our enemies were making. Although the surf still ran high, boats had obviously been ferrying supplies almost continuously from the ships to the shore, and we watched now as men unloaded two more. The first carried the weaponry and ammunition we expected. The other was laden with timber and tools, which were being added to large piles of other building materials that had already been beached. The presence of so many men and the growing store of supplies suggested what I had feared from the beginning — the siege we were anticipating would be lengthy and fierce.

I glanced at Guillaume. His expression told me what I already knew. We needed to get this information back to our leaders as soon as possible.

A stick cracked somewhere to our right.

Guillaume and I pulled back into the tall ferns growing alongside the brook as more than a dozen redcoats made their way toward our position, their muskets shouldered. I could hear them chatting as they drew closer, their words as unfamiliar to me as the letters on the Porte Dauphine plaque were to Guillaume.

Guillaume and I froze. Although our muskets were primed and ready to fire, the two of us would be no match for so many soldiers, and it was crucial that we return to Louisbourg with our report. As the soldiers approached closer still, I controlled my breathing to prevent even the slight movements of my chest from disturbing the ferns and betraying our presence. Guillaume, who lay a hand-width from me, was doing the same.

When the men were just steps away, I caught a sudden movement. A flick. And then another — the forked tongue of a thick brown snake slithering away from the redcoats' boots. Coiling beneath the ferns, it was far longer than my arm and thicker than the barrel of my musket. None of the reptiles in Île Royale were poisonous, but that was not what worried me.

I slowly turned toward Guillaume, hoping he had not spied the snake. But he had, his face now white as parchment. I wanted to reach out to him, to place my hand on his shoulder and reassure him, but I dared not move.

At any moment I expected panic to get the better of him and send him fleeing, an expectation that only increased when the snake suddenly glided toward Guillaume's face. It was as though the creature was unaware of his presence, perhaps mistaking his motionless body for a fallen log. I knew we could not escape discovery now. Guillaume would not be able to contain his terror. He would bolt.

I gripped the musket that I feared I would shoot for the last time, and I thought of Marie-Claire. I pictured how she had looked when we parted that morning, her eyes dark and tear filled. I thought of her praying for our safety and I waited for the worst.

The snake continued to slither forward, its scaly surface brushing Guillaume's chin as it passed. His eyes grew saucer wide and he swallowed thickly, the sound like a too-ripe pear being squeezed in a fist.

In that final moment, as I prepared to leap from our hiding place to attack the redcoats, I was grateful that at least I would die there with my friend. We had grown up together in France, crossed the ocean together, served our king together. We had begun our new lives together in this unfamiliar land, and together we would end them here.

But death did not come.

The snake slithered off through the ferns, and the soldiers walked within an arm's reach of us and continued on their way, never knowing we were there.

* * *

"Are you certain?" asked the governor.

I felt awkward and tongue-tied in his presence, but Boudier had insisted that Guillaume and I share our findings with the war council in person. "*Oui*, Gouverneur Drucour," I said, wishing I had had time to wash before entering his apartments. I was afraid my soiled uniform might brush against his fine furnishings. "There were at least twelve thousand men camped at Pointe Platte. Probably more."

"And you agree with his estimate?" Drucour asked Guillaume.

"*Oui, Excellence*," he replied. "At least that many." While Guillaume had never learned to read, numbers were as real as rocks to him. "And the enemy is landing supplies all the time. Mostly building materials."

The governor nodded gravely. He turned to Boudier and the other officers. "The British will launch their attack from the high ground that surrounds us, so they will no doubt build batteries there to provide cover for their weapons."

"Their efforts will be wasted," came a voice from my left. Lieutenant Colonel Saint-Julhien. "Our cannons will blow those batteries to bits."

Governor Drucour shook his head. "Unfortunately, the British know the range of our weapons. We showed them the day you retreated from Anse de la Cormorandière when we fired over your soldiers' heads to keep our enemies from advancing. The British will surely build their batteries safely beyond that distance."

Saint-Julhien's face flushed crimson and he said no more.

Governor Drucour addressed the council again. "Fortunately, transporting their supplies from the coast will be no small matter, and then our enemies must build whatever batteries and redoubts they hope to use in their assault. That may give us some time before their forces are in place and fully prepared to attack. I have written to our leaders requesting assistance. I am hopeful it will arrive before the offensive begins. Until then, we have only one option open to us."

He turned to the map of Île Royale spread across the table in front of him. "Here is what we must do."

Chapter 7
June 12, 1758

Standing at the Bastion Maurepas overlooking the harbour, I cursed the fog that had drifted in from the sea the previous night and now wrapped around Louisbourg like a shroud.

"Pea soup could not be thicker," Guillaume growled.

He was right. Anything beyond a few steps from us was swallowed by the dense mist blanketing the town. It was more than a mere nuisance. It was a benefit to the British because it meant further delay in carrying out our orders.

Governor Drucour had asked his officers to form five special forces made up of volunteers from the Troupes de Terre battalions and the Compagnies Franches de la Marine. They were to make frequent sorties into the area surrounding Louisbourg to monitor enemy movements and, whenever possible, take prisoners who could be questioned for information. Guillaume and I had immediately volunteered, and our detachment had been assigned to learn how advanced the

British were in their efforts to prepare the hills beyond the town for attack. However, lacking sufficient visibility to move safely beyond Louisbourg's walls, we had been assigned other duties. Earlier that day, we had moved gunpowder from the Bastion du Roi to lime kilns near the Porte Maurepas. While this work was necessary to safeguard the powder from mortar fire, Guillaume and I were eager to discover what the British were accomplishing beyond the walls, and impatient to pass along any crucial information.

Because the higher ground west of the town made us vulnerable to attack, the governor had also requested that a frigate be anchored strategically in the harbour so it could fire upon the hillsides. Its guns would be able to target the areas beyond the reach of the bastions' cannons, thereby increasing our range. The *Aréthuse*, commanded by Jean Vauquelin, had already moved into position. Try as I might, though, I failed to see the ship through the fog in the harbour. Standing there with the mist swirling around us, I suddenly felt uneasy.

"Is something wrong?" asked Guillaume.

I cocked my head to one side, listening. "Do you hear anything?"

He, too, listened for a moment. "Only the creak of our ships at anchor. Why?"

I pointed toward the northeast. "I thought I heard movement out there."

"Just now?"

"Earlier, too."

He scowled. "Even British fools wouldn't try sailing into this harbour with the fog so thick."

I shook my head. "The sounds were more like movement on land. And digging."

Guillaume shrugged, turning to look where I had pointed. "Perhaps you heard the men posted on the island battery."

"Perhaps," I said, "but the sounds seemed more distant than that."

"Who can tell anything accurately in this murk?" he asked.

"*Touché,*" I nodded. "It was probably our comrades on the island."

A moment passed as we stood peering into the fog, listening. But the only sounds were the wash of waves against the shore and the creaking of our ships' rigging as they rose and fell. Yet still I felt uneasy.

Chapter 8
June 13, 1758

I worked feverishly beside the cannon at Pointe à Rochefort, my tired arms like lead, my ears ringing from the repeated blasts of the huge gun. Captain Boudier had once said that a twenty-four-pounder could be fired ninety to a hundred times a day, but surely this one had already surpassed that. I was exhausted, but there was no time to rest. Like my comrades beside me, I pressed on. We had no choice.

The previous afternoon, when the fog had finally lifted, I saw that my unease had been justified. The British had occupied Pointe à la Phare, the fist of land beyond the island battery that my comrades had abandoned days before. Given their positions, the British must have moved quietly to avoid detection.

When Drucour's war council learned what was happening, they issued orders for the gunners at Pointe à Rochefort to fire upon the British. It was crucial that they not be allowed to erect their own battery, since from there they could easily bombard both the island battery and our ships in the harbour, leaving us defenceless. By early evening our leaders were confident that the Rochefort guns had halted British efforts to establish themselves there.

But despite our barrage, dawn revealed that the British had continued working throughout the night, prompting Drucour to call for an all-out offensive against Pointe à la Phare. The cannons aboard our warships and those of the island battery had joined the Rochefort twenty-four-pounders in a massive assault.

With so many men required for such a large-scale bombardment, I had been reassigned to the Pointe à Rochefort battery to assist in supplying and arming the cannons. But I would rather have been accompanying Guillaume on the sortie that had been delayed by fog the previous day.

"I wish I were going with you," I had told him earlier that morning.

He'd nodded. "Just be sure that each of your shots finds it mark."

"I'll do my best," I said, forcing a grin. As he attached fresh cartridge boxes to his waist-belt, a chill swept over me, as though a cloud had momentarily blocked the sun. "Guillaume," I said, "you will take no chances, *oui*?"

He shrugged. "Wars are not won by careful men," he said.

I understood his meaning. And I knew that he would have the support of two dozen others, like Renard Gaston, who had stood waiting for Guillaume. Yet still I could not shake the feeling that something was amiss.

Guillaume laid a hand on my shoulder. "Ah, Sébastien," he had said, "who was it that forced you to finally speak to Marie-Claire two years ago?"

"You," I replied.

"And who accompanied you when you asked her father for her hand two weeks ago?"

"You," I repeated.

"And it is I who will be toasting you when you finally marry." He had hoisted his musket and touched his tricorne in a mock salute before turning to Renard. "Come, Renard. You and I must rout the British before Sébastien has second thoughts and withdraws his proposal."

The two had chuckled and I forced myself to join in their laughter before bidding them farewell.

But standing now at Pointe à Rochefort preparing the cannon for firing again, I had that same sense of misgiving. I shrugged it off, telling myself it was only because the British had surprised us at every turn. Rather than worrying about the future, I needed to concentrate on blasting the enemy at Pointe à la Phare into oblivion. Had I not promised Guillaume to make every shot true?

As I'd done all morning and afternoon, I picked up the sponge, a long staff with one end wrapped in lambskin, and repeatedly rammed it down the cannon's barrel. After scouring away dirt and smothering any sparks that might remain after the previous shot, I stood back as a comrade ladled powder down the barrel and added a wad of paper. Then I dropped in the cannonball and reached for the rammer, using it to drive the ball and the powder into the breech before nodding to the officer of the artillery.

Sergeant Gerard Fournier checked both the cannon's aim and its elevation. Satisfied, he lit the fuse, and the explosion that followed made the earth shudder. As the cannonball arced through the air toward Pointe à la Phare, I wondered how long the mortar in our battery's walls could withstand those vibrations. The masonry closest to the sea weakened even more quickly than the rest, and the battery at Pointe à Rochefort took the brunt of every storm from the northeast, the waves often crashing against the mortared stones.

As I did after every tenth shot, I took a moment to cool the cannon by dipping the lambskin into a pail of water before sponging the barrel clean. While I worked, I imagined Guillaume returning from the day's sortie, the usual grin on his face. Regardless of whatever danger he had encountered, he would no doubt weave it into a humorous tale as he had with our experience at Pointe Platte. No one realized how close we had come to death or capture that day, because Guillaume had exaggerated the size of the snake tenfold, along with his reaction to it, his face contorting with the telling. Even Renard, who seldom spoke, had begged him to tell the story again.

"Cease firing!" barked Captain Boudier.

Never had I welcomed two words more. The muscles in my back throbbed, but I ignored them. What mattered was that our offensive was over. Little could be seen across the harbour because of the smoke from the many guns we had fired from the island and Pointe à Rochefort batteries, as well as from our warships. However, even if only a portion of our shots had met their mark, Pointe à la Phare surely would be a threat no longer.

"Good work," said Captain Boudier to Sergeant Fournier, then extended the same praise to the rest of us. "All Louisbourg will be grateful for your efforts today."

After my comrades and I had cleaned the cannons and restocked the battery's supply of ammunition, Boudier selected four men to take the first watch, and then dismissed the rest of us. Most made their way toward the barracks, eager to fill their bellies or to sleep, but I hurried in a different direction.

Some minutes later, I reached the Porte Dauphine at the western end of the town and asked the guards on duty if the men from today's sortie had returned. They told me the group had yet to appear. I glanced at the lowering sun. Guillaume and the others should have been back by now. It would not be wise for them to remain beyond the town's walls after dark. I settled myself on a bench to wait.

I must have dozed, because I awoke with a start to the sounds of musket fire and shouts. The sun had all but disappeared, and the lengthening shadows had cast everything in a deep gloom. I leaped up, reaching for my musket as the sound of running feet approached the gate.

"*Ouvrez la porte!*" came panicked voices on the other side. "*Ouvrez la porte!*"

The guards at the gate looked toward the

sentry for confirmation, then raised the bar that held the gate closed. Easing it open partway, they stood back to allow nine soldiers to rush through before swinging it shut again. The arrivals' uniforms were nearly unrecognizable, all of them slick with what looked like mud. Some men bleeding freely from wounds collapsed on the ground. Others stood bent over, gasping, their hands on their knees.

Twenty-five soldiers had left Louisbourg that morning. Of the nine who had returned, none was Guillaume.

I spied Christophe Gilbert among the group and ran to him. "Christophe! What happened?"

Still wheezing, he drew himself up and turned to me. Blood streaming from a gash on his forehead covered much of his face. "We were driven into hiding." He gulped for air. "Shortly after we left."

"Driven?" I asked.

He nodded. "The hills beyond the town. They teem with the enemy." He wheezed again as he wiped blood from his eyes. "Twice we were nearly discovered. We hid in a marsh. Waited until the sun was setting. We hoped the shadows would mask our return."

"Where is Guillaume?"

Christophe's face crumpled. "As we made our way back — " He coughed, drew a ragged breath.

"A scouting party attacked. Killed six of our number outright." He paused, as if remembering the horror of those moments, then forced himself to continue. "Others were wounded. We fought hand-to-hand. I struggled with the one who gave me this." He pointed to the gash on his forehead. "Guillaume shot him before — " He coughed again. "Before he could finish the job."

"*Where* is Guillaume?" I repeated.

Christophe grimaced. "We dared not risk fighting longer. We ran, but Renard . . . " He looked away as if unable to continue.

Édouard Villeneuve stepped toward us and took up the story. "Renard was shot. Guillaume went back to hoist him up. I turned to help, but Guillaume waved me on."

"But where — "

"Guillaume shouted that we must keep going," Édouard explained. "We had to let our leaders know what we'd seen. He wouldn't let himself and Renard slow us down." Édouard looked at his muddy boots.

Christophe managed to speak again, his voice a little stronger. "The British kept firing. Men on either side of me fell. I ran, sure that at any moment a shot would take me too. When I was almost to the gate, I turned back. Guillaume lagged far behind, carrying Renard in his arms. I started back to help him, but he shouted for me to get inside. Then more muskets fired and he went down."

"We must go to him!" I cried, turning toward the gate. "He may still be — "

A hand grabbed my arm. "Sébastien," said Christophe, "it is no use. Guillaume is dead."

Interlude

July 26, 1758
9:42 a.m.

Marching at Major Loppinot's side, I nod at my comrades standing at their posts, their faces every bit as grim as my own. Every soldier within Louisbourg's now shattered walls is preparing for the final onslaught, yet each surely knows there can be only one outcome. Each understands that the breath he draws now is among the last he will ever take. Even the flag I hold seems to reflect the futility of our struggle. It hangs nearly motionless, its only movement the result of my footsteps on what remains of this cobblestone street. Living as we do by the sea, we are accustomed to winds driving the surf onto the rocks, but today there is none. It is as if the elements, too, have suffered defeat at British hands.

The face of every soldier we meet turns toward the flag I carry, eyes following it intently as we pass. I cannot help but wonder what my comrades now see in that rectangular field of white. Is it a memory of home? A life before Louisbourg? Or is it the afterlife they focus on now, imagining Paradise as an endless expanse of sun-washed clouds? Thoughts of the afterlife must surely have passed through each of their minds since the British made landfall seven weeks ago. They have witnessed enough deaths by now to remind them of their own mortality.

My fellow soldiers and I have fought valiantly, but all of our efforts to defend Louisbourg have been for naught. All of the men who have given their lives have done so in vain. As I walk beside the major now, the letter in his hand an impossible burden, I cannot help but think of Captain Boudier, Jacques Legrand, Renard Gaston, Édouard Villeneuve, Pierre Grimaud, Gerard Fournier and the many others like them who died in their service to King Louis. Most of all, though, I think of Guillaume, whose body lies somewhere beyond these ruined walls. No better friend could a man have had. No better comrade could a soldier have fought beside. Christophe Gilbert, who now bears a jagged scar on his forehead from that day, knows this. Yet his physical scar is no more real, no more painful than the one I carry in my heart as I think of my closest friend lost forever. There is one consolation in knowing that my own death will surely follow the delivery of Drucour's letter — my soul will soon accompany Guillaume's.

That consolation, however, offers me little comfort when I think of the civilians who will join us. I struggle against tears at the thought of Marie-Claire being killed in the coming barrage, her body mangled by mortars. The idea that one so innocent, so filled with life, should have it stolen from her in so brutal a manner fills me with fury. But there is nothing I can do to prevent it. The die has been cast. I can only hold on to the memory of my last moments with her and pray that both our ends will be swift.

Before meeting Major Loppinot this morning to perform my duty as flag-bearer, I returned once more to the casemates in the Bastion du Roi where Marie-Claire, her mother and her sister have taken refuge with other women and children. Monsieur Desbarats, who once intimidated me with his feigned gruffness, was killed four days ago when a British mortar bomb struck his home. While Marie-Claire has struggled with this loss, the other two Desbarats women have been consumed by it, wearing their grief like a yoke whose weight grows heavier with each passing hour. But Marie-Claire has drawn from a wellspring of strength I had no idea she possessed. She is no longer a daughter and a sister. She has become nurse and mother to both sister and parent. She takes it upon herself each day to ensure that they eat at least a little, and she does her best to raise their spirits, as much as any can be raised in this rubble-strewn town.

Marie-Claire and I both know, though, that her efforts will see no return. Like everyone else here, the lives of Louisbourg's women and children mean nothing to the British dogs. Like everyone else, they are as good as dead.

In our final moments together this morning, I fought to keep emotion from overwhelming me. I had only one thing left to offer her: my courage. Holding her in my arms, I once more professed my love and promised that soon we would be together forever.

Like Guillaume and so many others before and after him, we will all be together before night falls again on Île Royale.

Chapter 9
June 15, 1758

War does not recognize grief. It does not offer soldiers the luxury of time to mourn. There is only duty.

The days following the failed sortie were a blur of activity. There were moments when I almost forgot that Guillaume was gone, moments when the hollowness in my chest felt more like hunger than the grief I knew it to be. Sorrow had become part of the landscape of my life, the backdrop against which everything else unfolded.

Despite our heavy bombardment of Pointe à la Phare, the British continued to dig in there. Adding to our woes, three columns of enemy soldiers were rumoured to be advancing toward Louisbourg. As a result, every soldier within the town's walls was on high alert, and yesterday our drummers beat the *générale*, warning everyone that the British were coming. We lined the ramparts surrounding the town, vigilant for any sound or movement as we waited for the enemy to appear. By eleven o'clock that night, however, they still had not.

Some of us were allowed to return to our barracks, but no sooner had I drifted into an uneasy sleep than the *générale* roused me. I leaped from bed and joined my comrades on the wall again but, as before, the enemy was nowhere to be seen. Eventually we returned once more to the barracks, only to hear the *générale* a third time.

As we took our positions on the wall yet again, many of our company had begun to question whether the information about the planned attack was reliable. Even our leaders were dubious. One officer speculated that the rumoured invasion was only a ploy on the part of the British to unsettle us. If so, it was achieving its goal. By then our nerves were frayed, and lack of sleep had put all of us on edge.

Arriving at my post on the wall this morning, I let my tired eyes wander over what remained of our company, struggling not to show the emotion I felt at Guillaume's absence. I forced myself to direct all my attention on Captain Boudier.

"I know I speak for all of us," Boudier began, "when I say that the loss of our comrades two days ago weighs heavy on our hearts." He glanced at me and I nodded, swallowing around the lump that rose in my throat. "But," he continued, "we cannot allow their deaths to undermine our resolve.

Nor can we allow them to go unavenged." He scanned the company, allowing his words to hang in the air for a moment. "It's now more important than ever that we keep the enemy from breaching our walls. We must stand strong and hold firm against them."

I understood the captain's purpose — to rally our spirits in the face of crumbling morale — but his task was unrealistic at best, impossible at worst. Thanks to Édouard, Christophe and others who had survived the failed sortie, all of us knew that the forces now gathering beyond our walls vastly outstripped our own. We could not possibly fend off the British forever.

"I bring good news," Captain Boudier went on. "Gouverneur Drucour has received word that the battalion led by Charles Deschamps de Boishébert is now nearing Louisbourg. He brings with him twelve hundred men, and they shall reach the town any day now."

Boudier's news was indeed heartening for many. Some men cheered while others raised their muskets in the air. I, too, welcomed this information, but I could not help but wonder how Boishébert and his men were going to avoid detection or capture with thousands of British soldiers occupying the vicinity. And even if they did make it this far, how could they penetrate the stranglehold the British now had on Louisbourg? Even assuming that those twelve hundred men made it safely through our gates, would they be enough to turn the tide in our favour? For every Frenchman who fell, there seemed to be ten enemy soldiers wading into the breach.

No, I was not cheered by Boudier's report. But many of my comrades grasped this information like a lifeline, drawing strength from it and, more importantly, hope. Having no wish to take that from them, I kept my doubts to myself.

But someone had noticed nonetheless.

* * *

"You don't seem encouraged by Boudier's news," said Christophe, the bandage on his forehead covering an angry slash of puckered red flesh.

We brought the wagon to a halt. Along with several others in our company, we had been assigned to remove more gunpowder from the casemates of the Bastion du Roi, this time taking it to the ice house. Others had already been making some structures bombproof by stacking bags of dirt to reinforce them. While those efforts would no doubt make them safer, nothing would withstand a direct hit from enemy mortar fire. Nothing.

I shrugged in response to Christophe's comment

as, together, we hoisted a barrel of gunpowder from the wagon and set it carefully on the ground. I had no wish to share my misgivings. "Twelve hundred reinforcements will surely be welcome, will they not?" I asked.

"If they reach us," he muttered. He sounded skeptical, and why wouldn't he be? Had he not seen first-hand the extent of the enemy's advance? Seen comrades cut down while obtaining that information? Watched Guillaume die?

I suddenly wanted to give in to hopelessness, wanted to toss aside my musket and waist-belt, watch my cartridge boxes fall where they might as I walked away from my duty. More than anything, I wanted to spend whatever days or hours or minutes remained with Marie-Claire.

I paused, actually considering this mutiny as I leaned against the barrel of gunpowder.

And then I thought of the casemates at the Bastion du Roi and the people they would shelter when the British finally launched their attack — the women and children of Louisbourg. My Marie-Claire would be among them. Perhaps she would be fortunate enough to survive the days ahead, but only if I and others like me did our part.

I glanced sharply at Christophe. "Only God

knows if Boishébert and his battalion will reach us," I said. "But even if they don't, we must do everything in our power to be ready for the enemy when they come."

"But what if everything in our power isn't enough?" asked Christophe.

"It has to be," I said simply, then repeated those words as much for myself and Marie-Claire as for Christophe. "It has to be."

Chapter 10
June 18, 1758

"Is it *true*, you worthless scoundrel?" roared a voice ahead of me on Rue de l'Étang.

"Please, sir, I — "

"Answer me!" the voice roared again. "Is it *true*?"

I had just finished my watch and was stiff from having stood at my post in the damp June air, cold fog swirling about me. The summer solstice was almost upon us, yet the weather continued to feel more like that of early spring. I felt chilled to the bone and looked forward to a hot bowl of stew and then taking to my bed, but not before seeing Marie-Claire. With the garrison on high alert, one watch now seemed to blur into the next and then the next, and it was difficult to steal more than a few moments to spend with her. But it was those moments that filled me with a sense of purpose, gave me the strength I needed in the face of the massive forces gathering beyond our walls. And during those few moments with her, I was able to ignore the sorrow that hung on me like shackles each time I thought of Guillaume.

It was her father's house that I was approaching

when the raised voices on the street ahead of me caught my attention. Édouard stood outside the Hôtel de la Marine, an inn where many of the garrison's soldiers had spent their off-duty time in the past. Even now, under threat of imminent attack, some managed to slip into the inn to drown their troubles with drink. Édouard was one of those. Since his participation in the failed sortie five days earlier, he had often stumbled back to the barracks, his eyes red, his manner surly. Judging from his appearance now, I suspected that this evening would be no different.

His face a twisted mask of rage, he loomed over a young man cowering before him. Clearly a servant, the young man glanced repeatedly around him, as if unwilling to call attention to himself. A disturbance in the street, especially now, would not be tolerated by the town guard.

I made my way toward them. Édouard's face was flushed from the rum he had drunk, and his body swayed unsteadily above the cobblestones.

"You miserable spawn of a weasel," he hissed. "By God, you shall tell me the truth or I will — "

"Édouard," I said as I reached the pair, *"quel est le problème?"*

He whirled toward me, his red eyes narrowing to slits before he recognized me. "Sébastien," he said, then belched, the sound abrupt and harsh in the evening air. "This rogue serves in Drucour's apartments."

"Surely that can't be such an offence," I said lightly, trying to defuse his anger.

He blinked as he considered my comment. "No," he snorted. "I overheard him talking inside," he said, nodding at the door of the Hôtel de la Marine. He prodded the youth in the chest. "Tell my comrade here what you said."

The youth's brow furrowed in apology. "I was wrong to speak of Gouvernour Drucour's business," he told Édouard. "Forgive me."

"You will forgive my knuckles against your teeth," snarled Édouard, "if you keep me waiting a moment longer."

The youth's eyes widened as he turned to me. "I serve Gouverneur and Madame Drucour," he said quickly. "I helped prepare a basket for Madame today."

None of this was of interest to me, and I wanted nothing more than to continue on my way to Marie-Claire. But before I could say as much, Édouard spoke again. "Tell him the contents of that basket," he ordered.

The young man checked up and down the street before he spoke. "Fifty bottles of Burgundy wine," he said, his voice barely audible.

"And just who was this wine for?" demanded Édouard.

A pained expression flickered across the young man's face. "Major General Amherst."

My jaw dropped. "The British commander?"

"*Oui*," he confirmed, his voice little more than a whisper.

Édouard turned from the young man to me. "Apparently," he snarled, "Madame Drucour serves the enemy now. She caters to the man leading the attack against us, the very man responsible for the deaths of Renard and Guillaume and — "

"The wine," the youth ventured to explain. "It was in response to the gift the major general sent her yesterday."

"Gift?" Édouard and I asked in unison.

"*Oui*," the young man replied. "The British commander sent her two pineapples."

Édouard's eyes widened, as mine must have. Neither of us had ever seen a pineapple, much less held one, but I had heard stories of their exotic flavour. Commoners like Édouard and myself would live our entire lives without once tasting such a delicacy, yet the governor and his wife had received *two* from the very man bent on destroying us all. Guillaume surely would have had something scathing to say about *that*.

"The pineapples arrived following a communication Drucour sent to Amherst," said the youth.

"Communication?" I asked.

He nodded. "Drucour was inquiring about the health of our men who were taken prisoner the day the British made landfall."

"And what was the British dog's response?" growled Édouard.

"Assurance that they were being cared for. Afterwards, he sent the pineapples to Madame Drucour." The young man shrugged. "That is all I know."

Scowling, Édouard gestured roughly for him to leave. The young man immediately obliged and, watching him scurry away, Édouard muttered, "Pineapples!" Belching again, he turned once more toward the inn and disappeared inside.

* * *

"Perhaps the gift of the pineapples was an act of courtesy," said Marie-Claire after I told her what had taken place in front of the inn. "Leaders can still be gentlemen during wartime. Even the British." Her shining eyes reflected something I'd not seen since I had asked for her hand in marriage seventeen days earlier — an openness, an expectation that the future was unfolding as it should.

I had not intended to share the story with her, but since Guillaume's death, she'd grown more anxious

86

for my safety, fearful that I, too, might fall victim to enemy fire. Because my delay had worried her, I'd told her of seeing Édouard outside the Hôtel de la Marine, exaggerating — as I knew Guillaume would have — lighter aspects of the servant's story. My purpose was merely to make Marie-Claire smile, but my account evoked a very different response. She drew from it a reason to hope.

"Surely," she said now, "those pineapples demonstrate the enemy's compassion and good-will. If their numbers are as great as everyone claims them to be, they could have overpowered Louisbourg long before this. Perhaps, Sébastien, that is no longer their intention."

I understood her desire to believe that our situation was not as grim as I knew it to be. I understood her need to have hope in the face of what I knew was certain doom. For this reason, I did not share my own interpretation of the enemy's gift to the Drucours — that it was less an act of courtesy than a reminder of the severe threat we faced. While French ships carrying much-needed supplies were blockaded from Louisbourg's harbour, the British had unlimited access to whatever they wished, even goods as exotic as pineapples. The enemy was strangling us before inflicting the final blow.

Chapter 11
June 19, 1758

"Press on, men!" shouted Captain Boudier as more British cannon fire tore the air.

Although the weather was no warmer than the day before, sweat rivered down my face. I worked as fast as I could alongside my comrades, once more arming the cannons at the Pointe à Rochefort battery. All of us knew that, with each new shot they fired, the British were finding their range. Their last one had reached the farthermost end of the spit of land where we now stood, the explosion sending dirt and debris high into the air and making the ground quiver beneath our feet.

Plunging the lambskin rammer into the barrel of the cannon, I once more looked toward Pointe à la Phare half a league across the harbour. Even in the waning daylight, we could see the results of the enemy's continued efforts there because the cursed fog had finally lifted. Pointe à la Phare was now a *British* battery whose cannons and howitzers were trained on the island battery, the town and our ships.

Our leaders' worst fears had been realized. Having constructed their own battery on the north side of the harbour, the British could now bombard the seaward side of Louisbourg without having to put their ships in danger of our guns. Now it was our own ships at anchor in the harbour that were in jeopardy. More than once during the past hour, a shot aimed at them had nearly hit its mark, falling just short and sending sheets of water cascading over the decks. Our naval officers had returned fire, but it was only a matter of time before one or more of those ships fell victim to British artillery.

I heard a low whistle beside me. "That one was close," said Sergeant Fournier as Christophe hoisted another cannonball and dropped it into the barrel. After grabbing the rammer and driving the ball and gunpowder into the breech, I looked where he was nodding — a ship, its spars now dripping from the deluge.

"The *Entreprenant*," Fournier remarked as he rechecked the cannon's aim and elevation before lighting the fuse. "What a loss that would have been."

Christophe grunted. "Mark my words," he muttered, then paused as we waited for the fuse to ignite the powder. When the explosion had echoed into the distance, he continued. "If those ships aren't moved farther out of range, it's only a matter of time before they are *all* lost."

Christophe sounded as if defeat were inevitable. And now in the face of what the enemy had achieved at Pointe à la Phare, how could any of us think otherwise? But I shrugged off that thought, swallowed the feeling that threatened to choke me. No soldier worth his salt could afford to give in to pessimism. I turned toward the ocean, knowing I would see the British blockade, yet hoping the horizon that stretched before me might offer fresh hope.

What I saw made my heart leap.

"Capitaine Boudier!" I shouted.

Speaking to my comrades at another cannon, he turned to me, scowling at my interruption.

"Excusez-moi, capitaine," I said as I hurried toward him, "but isn't that *Echo* approaching?" I pointed eastward, my heart racing. It had been ten days since *Echo* had slipped from the harbour under cover of darkness with *Comète* and *Bizarre*. The ship could not have reached France in that time, let alone make the return journey, but perhaps its captain had found reinforcements elsewhere.

"Look!" I exclaimed to my comrades as Boudier raised his telescope. "*Echo* returns!"

The soldiers standing with me in the battery froze, their eyes now trained with mine on the horizon. One of them raised a cheer, which was soon taken up as others recognized the ship in the distance, its bow pointed in our direction as it rode the waves toward Louisbourg. Like me, they scanned the horizon for the ships *Echo* was surely leading, wondering when her guns would engage the square-riggers blocking the harbour.

"De l'Espérance!"

I turned toward Boudier and my own cheer died on my lips. His face was flat. Before I could ask what was wrong, he handed me the eyepiece.

Peering through it, I saw what he had seen.

Echo now flew the flag of King George.

She had been captured.

Chapter 12
June 25, 1758

Standing on the rampart watching *Echo* sail across the mouth of the harbour yet again, I thought of the enemy sailors aboard her and imagined their smug satisfaction at flying the flag of Britain above a French vessel. Their purpose was clear. They were flaunting their prize in our faces.

And their action was achieving its desired result. Morale had suffered a staggering blow. Christophe was no longer alone in talking about the hopelessness of our situation. Muttering could often be heard among soldiers in every company as they debated our chances of repelling the British once they mounted an all-out assault on the town.

The promised reinforcements led by Charles Deschamps de Boishébert had not arrived, and Drucour's letters to the Minister of the Marine requesting additional support from France could not possibly bring us the help we needed in time. And despite our valiant attempts to destroy the British battery at Pointe à la Phare, we had failed.

In fact, the very opposite was true. Continuing to fire from there, the British had managed to silence most of our island battery's guns. Although those remaining on the ruined island still launched the occasional mortar, they had little effect on our enemies.

Under constant bombardment, those on the island battery could make no repairs, and our ability to keep the British from sailing into the harbour had been greatly weakened. Making matters worse, our warships — as Christophe had predicted — had changed position. To escape the barrage from Pointe à la Phare, they had raised anchor four days ago and moved as far inside the harbour as the water's depth permitted, which limited their effectiveness in defending the harbour entrance.

There had been talk that the ships' commanders had once again approached Governor Drucour requesting permission to leave Louisbourg, and Édouard had taken it upon himself to get to the bottom of this rumour. Once again spotting the governor's servant in the Hôtel de la Marine, Édouard had waited for the youth to leave and then followed him into the street. It took little of Édouard's persuasive ability to force the young man to tell what he knew — the Marquis des Gouttes had, indeed, gone to the governor's apartments early on June 22 and told Drucour that, with enemy artillery now firing from Pointe à la Phare, our ships were sure to be lost. With this a certainty, des Gouttes passionately argued that the governor allow some of the warships to sail away that night. He also recommended that, following the warships' departure, other French ships be sunk in the narrow channel at the harbour entrance so that their masts and spars would effectively block the British vessels from entering. Only such a move could prevent them from bombarding the town from within the harbour.

The governor's servant had been reluctant to say more but, given that the young man was well-fortified with rum, Édouard had managed to ferret out even more information from him. The servant had been within earshot when the governor called a special meeting of the war council later that day. After much discussion, the council's members had decided to allow two warships to sail for France, and des Gouttes had chosen *Entreprenant* and *Célèbre* to leave that evening under cover of darkness. Once they were gone, six ships would be sunk to block the channel, three of them warships and three large merchant ships.

I had only to look now toward the innermost

part of the harbour to see that none of this had taken place — all of our ships were still at anchor. Édouard shared with me the servant's suspicion that the governor had changed his mind and rescinded the order, but I wondered if the weather had played a greater part in this turn of events — the night this was to happen, the fog had returned and the wind had dropped, making it impossible for the ships to leave.

"Attention!"

I turned to see Corporal Grimaud salute Captain Boudier, who was approaching the company on the wall. Boudier's brow was furrowed.

"Mes amis," Boudier began, and I was surprised by his familiarity. He had never before addressed us as friends. I stifled a groan, certain that our situation had worsened even more.

"Now that the island battery has been silenced," said Boudier, "there is nothing to stop the British from advancing and establishing other batteries around the harbour."

No one said anything. After all, the captain had merely stated the obvious. But there was a finality and resignation in Boudier's words that we had not heard before. He suddenly looked far older than his years, but he squared his shoulders before he resumed speaking. "Our immediate concern is that hill." He pointed in its direction. "Perhaps an impossible task, but we cannot permit the British to entrench themselves there."

My eyes traced the hill that overlooked the town. It was less than a quarter league from the Bastion Dauphin and the Porte Dauphine. Should the British establish a battery within such close range, they could inflict major damage. Not only that, artillery there could easily offer protection for British soldiers building batteries even closer to the town.

"A scout has just returned with news of intense activity near the hill," Boudier continued. "Our leaders suspect that the British plan to send a large force there — possibly as early as tomorrow. We must do everything in our power to drive them back." He scanned the company. I wondered if he was seeing the faces before him or the absences of the men he had already lost. "Two other companies have already been assigned to hold the hill. They will head out before first light tomorrow. I have volunteered to lead the sortie."

A murmur rippled through the men, and while I could not make out their spoken words, I suspected that the thoughts of my comrades were the same as my own. We could not stand by as our captain undertook such a perilous mission. Just as he had never asked of us anything he would not do himself, neither would we allow him to attempt such a task without us by his side.

"*Capitaine!*" came Édouard's voice. "We, too, will drive those British dogs back!"

Other voices joined his, my own included. If I was to die, I had no wish to wait on this wall for the British to pummel us with cannon fire. I would strike now and avenge Guillaume's death. I would kill as many of the enemy as I could before they cut me down.

I looked around me as the shouts mounted. Even Christophe, who had long been forecasting our defeat, bellowed with the rest. Our voices echoed along the ramparts and out over the harbour, where occasional artillery fire continued. For a moment I imagined Guillaume's voice raised with our own. His shouts would have been loudest of all.

I watched as Captain Boudier's eyes travelled over the group, the corners of his mouth betraying the hint of a smile. After a moment, he raised his right hand and our cheers evaporated as we stood waiting for him to speak. Finally he said, "No greater reward can an officer desire than the loyalty of his men. Regardless of what happens tomorrow, I am honoured that you will be at my side." He saluted us, then turned and left the rampart.

Watching him go, I immediately thought of Marie-Claire. More than anything, I wanted to see her, wanted to tell her yet again how much I loved her. Because I was certain I would never have the opportunity to do so again.

But it was for this very reason I could not go to her. Even if I chose not to speak of tomorrow's mission, she might see on my face its futility. I could not burden her with the certainty of my death.

I would not.

Chapter 13
June 26, 1758

We left the town through thinning fog, the air heavy with the acrid stink of gunpowder and scorched timbers. Creeping through the semidarkness, my comrades and I were alert for the slightest sound or movement that might betray the enemy's presence. So far we had seen no evidence of the troops predicted to be advancing toward the hill to the southwest of us, but we were also prepared for whatever British soldiers were already in the area. It was likely that those who had killed Guillaume and Renard and so many others were camped somewhere nearby, and we had no desire to stumble upon them. The scouts had not yet returned and, despite having heard no weapon fire, we couldn't be certain they hadn't been captured. Or killed.

As we approached the hilltop, I tried to keep my mind on the moment, tried not to recall the countless times Guillaume and I had walked this same slope as we hunted for game. But, of course, images of his grinning face and echoes of his laughter filled my head. I struggled to keep them at bay, forcing myself to focus on the mission at hand. Suddenly the brush to my right exploded with movement and I spun toward it, my finger nearly squeezing the trigger of my musket before I saw there was no danger. We had surprised a partridge, which whirled into the air and then fell to earth, running erratically through the grass and dragging one wing in an attempt to lead us away from her nest. I wondered whether I and my comrades might have to use a similar tactic this day. But I quickly shook that thought aside. Regardless of the size of the enemy force, there could be no energy wasted on anything other than attack. Regardless of the odds stacked against us, we had to strike a decisive blow against the British. We could not let them take this hill, no matter who might be killed in the process.

Ahead of us, Captain Boudier froze and his right arm shot into the air. Each of the men in the sortie halted in mid-step behind him. A moment passed before I realized that I was holding my breath, waiting for whatever sign he would give us. Another moment passed, then he motioned us forward once again.

I glanced to my left to see Christophe and Édouard moving almost as one, their expressions as grim as my own. All of the men under Boudier's command understood the importance of today's mission. It was as vital as the battle nearly three weeks earlier when we had tried to keep the enemy from making landfall. The failure of that mission had brought us to this very moment. If the British established themselves on this hill overlooking the town, they could fire upon us at will. It would be the beginning of the end for Louisbourg and for everyone who called the port home.

Conscious now of Édouard's sure-footed movements beside me, I recalled my surprise when he had returned to the barracks last night with good news. I usually expected him to appear in the doorway reeling and reeking of rum but, in fact, he had spent his off-duty time accompanying Christophe to the garrison hospital, where they had visited Jacques Legrand. Still recovering from his stomach wound, l'Enfant was no longer at death's door. That good news had cheered everyone in our company.

Guillaume, too, would have been happy that Jacques survived. I thought of him carrying the boy to safety in those final minutes of our retreat from Anse de la Cormorandière. That memory, in turn, led me to think of Guillaume staggering under Renard's weight as he had headed toward the Porte Dauphine, only to be cut down by a British musket.

I wondered if Édouard was thinking now about his last time beyond the town's walls, and I turned toward him just as the first rays of sunshine touched the hillside. In that moment, Édouard's eyes met my own and he nodded as if he knew what I was thinking.

And then a musket ball smashed through his forehead, driving his body to the ground.

The hillside echoed with weapon fire from both sides as we dove for cover, Captain Boudier shouting orders above the din. Judging from the number of muskets now shooting at us, we were facing hundreds of enemy *fusiliers*, even more than had been predicted. Clearly the British had every intention of maintaining control of the hill we had sworn to wrench from their grasp. I took aim at an enemy soldier whose uniform had become a red beacon in the sudden sunshine. I pulled the trigger and prayed my aim would be true. It was. The redcoat crumpled to the ground.

I reloaded and squeezed the trigger again, repeating the process over and over, even as I heard comrades along the hillside being struck by musket fire.

Our position on higher ground began to work

to our advantage. Despite being outnumbered, those of us remaining drew beads on enemy soldiers again and again. Few of our shots missed their mark, and the British began to draw back, regrouping farther down the hillside. One redcoat struggled to carry another who had been wounded, and I knew I could easily take the life of either. Thinking of Guillaume, I clenched my jaw and aimed my musket first at one and then the other, and I touched the trigger. But I could not bring myself to squeeze it. Instead, I looked for other targets.

"Attention!" Captain Boudier shouted above the blasts of muskets on both sides. He clasped his right arm with his left hand, blood seeping between his fingers. *"Attention!"* he called again. "They will try to outflank us on — "

A hole suddenly appeared in his uniform above his waist-belt. Dropping his musket, he clutched his stomach with his free hand. Even amid the clamour, I could hear him gasp, yet he struggled to continue speaking. "You must — " he began again, blood bubbling from his mouth " — keep them from approaching from — "

Another shot caught him in the throat and he staggered backwards before dropping to the ground.

It was only then that I saw what he had been

trying to tell us — a wave of redcoats was surging over the hill. I struggled to remain calm as I reloaded, struggled to keep my hands steady as shots whizzed past my head. Drawing my musket up to fire again, I took aim and squeezed the trigger. But I was the one who fell.

Chapter 14
June 28, 1758

Even with my eyes closed, I knew the hands holding my own were Marie-Claire's, warm and soft against my rough skin. I could feel their gentle pressure as she held my left hand between both of hers. I opened my eyes.

"Sébastien," she whispered, reaching forward and stroking my cheek as tears rolled down her own. "I feared you would never waken."

She was sitting in a chair beside the bed where I lay. But not in the barracks. I was in a large room, its many beds filled with bandages. And then I realized there were men beneath those bandages. I was in the King's Hospital. Beyond it, sounds of artillery fire punched the air.

I tried raising my free hand to wipe away her tears, but pain seared my chest, drawing the breath from my lungs in a sudden gasp.

"*Attention*," she whispered. "You must not try to move."

"How long — " I began, but words would not come easily.

Marie-Claire, however, could guess my meaning. *"Deux jours,"* she said.

"Deux?" I croaked. Surely it was not possible. Had I really lain unconscious for two days? How had I gotten here? And what had happened to my comrades?

My last moment suddenly swam into memory. I saw again the redcoats flanking us, flowing like a red tide over the top of that hill, cutting down all in their path — Captain Boudier, Édouard and so many others falling around me. Corporal Grimaud took three hits, one to a leg and two to his chest, yet he continued to fire before being brought down finally by a fourth. Had any of them survived? There was so much I wanted to ask her, so much I wanted to know, but already I could feel consciousness slipping from me like water through my fingers. I tried to summon the strength to voice my thoughts, but my vision clouded . . .

Chapter 15
June 30, 1758

"S'il te plaît, Sébastien, you must try to eat more," Marie-Claire urged as she held the spoon to my lips. "You need to rebuild your strength."

When I had regained consciousness two days earlier, the surgeon-major told me I had lost considerable blood, both from my wound and the surgery that had repaired it. But I chafed at the thought of lying in bed while my comrades continued to die at the hands of our enemies.

Marceau Lafontaine, a wounded comrade who had been brought into the hospital after me, confirmed what I feared — the British now controlled the hill, and the constant artillery fire we heard came from our cannons repeatedly bombarding their position. Our leaders hoped the barrage would prevent the enemy from establishing their battery atop the hill, so every available man was needed to maintain the assault. For this reason I believed I should be on the western rampart loading our twenty-four-pounders, a thought I had already shared with the surgeon-major. He had not agreed, and so I was forced to remain in bed, forced to listen to the boom of artillery as I drank the broth that Marie-Claire spooned into me.

Musket shot had torn through my chest just below my right collarbone, and I could barely move without pain knifing through me. If not for the tincture of opium given me four times each day, I doubt I would have been able to move at all. At least the musket ball had struck no vital organs and had passed cleanly through my body. I would recover fully and in less time than others such as Jacques, who had twice been struck with fever when his wound became infected. However, the surgeon-major had recently told him that he should finally be well enough to leave the hospital, perhaps within the week.

Marie-Claire had been at my bedside every day since I'd been carried back inside the wall. Christophe, one of the few from our company to escape injury, had slung my unconscious body over his shoulder before making his way back to the Porte Dauphine, refusing to put me down even as enemy musket fire increased. This I had learned from Marceau, who'd managed to limp back from the hill with a musket ball in his thigh. He told me it was surely rage that had given Christophe the strength to carry me so far, rage that had arisen from seeing his friend Édouard brutally killed an arm's length from him. I had not yet seen Christophe to thank him — others said that he now spent every free moment in the Hôtel de la Marine. However, it would be my first act as soon as I was permitted to leave my bed.

Each day Marie-Claire brought with her further accounts of the siege. None of what she shared was good, especially the news of the *Capricieux* receiving a direct hit from British cannon fire last night. The loss had devastated Louisbourg's already crumbling morale. Even worse than the warship's loss was what it now meant. The *Capricieux* and other vessels had been moved to the far end of the harbour, yet still she had been hit. It was only a matter of time before the other ships would be destroyed by enemy artillery, leaving us with no naval defence whatsoever.

Desperate to keep the British from sailing into the harbour, Governor Drucour had apparently revisited the Marquis de Gouttes's recommendation to sink some of our remaining ships in the channel. The previous day he had ordered the captains of the *Apollon*, the *Fidèle*, the *Chèvre* and the *Ville de Saint Malo* to scuttle their vessels. Their crews were reassigned to the garrison, but Marie-Claire had heard rumours that many of them were drinking heavily, rumours that worried many of the townspeople, who were already concerned for Louisbourg's defence.

As Marie-Claire told me this news, I could see that my efforts to shield her from the hopelessness of Louisbourg's situation had been useless. No one could ignore the despair that grew stronger each day. Marie-Claire knew as well as I that the town was doomed. Yet neither of us put that thought into words. Each of us would continue to pretend for the other that our forces would still prevail. We would cling to this pretense for as long as we could. The alternative, to admit to the certainty of our deaths at the hands of our enemies, served no purpose.

I reached for her hand, grimacing at the pain this movement caused me, and squeezed it. "Don't worry," I told her. "We shall yet be saved."

"I know," she lied in return.

Chapter 16
July 6, 1758

I sat on the edge of my bed, waiting restlessly for Marie-Claire to arrive. The surgeon-major had reluctantly given me permission to leave the hospital that evening, and I was eager to return to whatever duty would be assigned me, but not before I shared this news with her. Even if I was still too weak to arm the cannons, I could keep watch, could I not? I could sound the alarm. My wound was far from healed, but I was a soldier in the Compagnies Franches de la Marine, and I would serve as best I could. Truthfully, I did not welcome the command of another officer, but I suspected I would not be in his service for long. The British noose was tightening around the town. The redcoats had nearly completed construction of their battery on the hill to the west, despite our continual bombardment. Surely the enemy assault from that position was not far off.

I shrugged aside that gloomy prediction as Marie-Claire came through the doorway. She had refused to let the siege keep her from me, coming twice daily to the hospital despite the ever-present sounds of artillery fire. Like so many times before, I felt my heart swell at the sight of her moving toward me, pausing briefly at several of the beds to greet the wounded she had come to know. One was Jacques, who seemed to look forward to her arrival as much as I.

Her face fell the moment she noticed my uniform. Although she had said nothing about it, I knew she had dreaded the prospect of my release.

She forced a smile. "You are well at last, Sébastien," she said.

I took her hands in mine, ignoring the sudden twinge in my chest. *"Oui,"* I told her, "well at last." I reached for my tricorne, then held out my arm for her to take. "May I accompany you to your door?" I asked gallantly. It was the first request I had made of her two years earlier, a request Guillaume had suggested.

A sudden blast of mortar fire halted us in our steps, and a moment later a nearby explosion shook the room. Plaster fell from the ceiling, and I drew Marie-Claire toward me to shield her. "They must fire from the new battery!" I shouted above a second explosion that seemed even closer. More plaster fell, this time in chunks, and a soldier lying on a bed to my left screamed in pain. "Out!" I shouted.

I tugged Marie-Claire's hand and together we hurried past the wounded, who now struggled to rise from their beds. I would return to assist them, but first I would take Marie-Claire to safety. Despite the pain in my chest, I continued to urge her forward, and we made it outside in moments. "To the Bastion du Roi!" I said. "You'll be safe in the casemates." Looking at the burning ruin of a building that had just been struck, I did not believe my own words, but there was no other option.

Another blast of mortar fire tore the air, and an incoming bomb whistled toward us. I gripped Marie-Claire's hand ever harder, pulling her with me, and then an explosion knocked us both to the ground.

I lay there trying to gather my senses, my ears ringing. The wound in my chest blazed with pain, but I had not been struck. I rolled slightly to see that Marie-Claire was unharmed, but she was equally dazed.

"Marie-Claire!" I moaned. "Get up!" I pushed myself to my feet, my chest afire with fresh agony as I drew her up beside me. She swayed unsteadily, but I could give her no time to get her bearings. I pulled her in the direction of the Bastion du Roi, with one look behind to see where the mortar bomb had struck. The hospital was in ruins.

Chapter 17
July 9, 1758

I scanned the troops lined up before the Porte de la Reine, impressed that nearly seven hundred men could wait so quietly for the order to leave. Although midnight had passed only an hour earlier, all of the men looked surprisingly alert, eager to accomplish their mission. They had to be. This was unlike any other sortie we'd undertaken.

Once more I wished I were accompanying them. I longed to strike a blow against the British that might avenge the deaths of Renard, Édouard, Captain Boudier, Corporal Grimaud and so many others. But mostly I longed to make our attackers pay for the killing of Guillaume. However, the officer leading the sortie, Lieutenant Colonel Marin, had denied my request to take part. The success of this mission depended on the element of surprise and the ability of each man to move quickly and to inflict maximum damage. My comrades would not be engaging the British with weapon fire. Instead, they would strike with bayonets. Marin hoped that, by killing in silence, our men would be able to attack several of the enemy camps dug in along the hillside before the British were even aware our troops had left the town. It was a bold plan, but boldness was required if we were to survive this siege.

Although I yearned to drive my own bayonet into the hearts of British soldiers, I could not. When the explosion at the hospital had thrown me to the ground, my wound had opened up again. Even now it continued to bleed sporadically.

I allowed my thoughts to turn to that moment. It was the people nearest the hospital's far end, where the bomb had struck, who'd been most vulnerable. Two were badly injured in the blast and two had died instantly, one of them Jacques. He had survived a life-threatening wound only to die in the very building where his life had been saved. And the man who had saved it, the surgeon-major, had died along with him. Even now, the bitter irony of it threatened to choke me, and once more I burned to strike back at the enemy.

I was disappointed by Marin's refusal to let me take part in tonight's attack, but I knew he was right. Yes, I had proven my skills as a marksman many times, but the success of tonight's mission hinged on strength and speed. And it was crucial that tonight's sortie be successful.

As our leaders had feared, the new British battery had provided them the very cover they needed to begin building entrenchments closer to the wall surrounding the town. Every man now standing before me at the Porte de la Reine knew that if those were completed, the British artillery would be able to target our remaining ships anchored in shallow water. The British needed these entrenchments even more now because the ships we had sunk in the channel blocked their own from entering the harbour. As a result, the enemy was focusing every resource on preparing for a sweeping attack from the landward side.

While morale had continued to flag in every company and battalion during the previous weeks, everyone had been encouraged by the success of *Aréthuse*, the ship under the command of Jean Vauquelin. In one night, the crew of *Aréthuse* had fired a hundred rounds from the harbour at the hill battery, severely disrupting work on their entrenchments. This welcome turn of events had given many of my comrades hope that the British could be stopped after all, and this was the task awaiting the men standing before me now.

The glow from torches mounted near the Porte de la Reine illuminated Lieutenant Colonel Marin as he moved to the front of the battalion. The group was comprised of men from every unit in Louisbourg. Once the soldiers had eliminated the enemy at each entrenchment, our labourers would destroy what the British had built.

It was important that no British scout who might be hidden near the Porte de la Reine overhear what was about to happen. Rather than speaking, Marin raised his arm and saluted the men. Each raised a silent salute in return. He turned to me and nodded. I raised the bar and drew open the gate, watching as he and his troops filed past, their boots treading softly on the damp ground. Among them was Sergeant Fournier, who had served in Captain Boudier's company long before Guillaume and I arrived in Louisbourg. He tipped his tricorne toward me as he passed, and I wondered if he was thinking of Boudier now, wondered if he wished he were following Boudier instead of Marin into the darkness. I had heard that the lieutenant colonel was a good leader, but none could compare with the captain, whose final thoughts had been not for himself but for the safety of his men. I nodded to Sergeant Fournier in return, all the while praying that he and the others would succeed in their mission.

Once all were beyond the wall, I closed the gate and took my position atop the rampart, straining to follow their progress toward the British battery. The new moon had barely begun to wax, casting very little light, but the stars provided just enough for me to distinguish the two columns of men from the landscape that stretched dark and silent around them. After a moment the columns split and then split again as individual groups targeted different entrenchments on the hillside.

Watching them move toward the enemy, I thought of the separation that had so distressed Marie-Claire during the past three days. She had gone willingly to the casemates of the Bastion du Roi, where her mother and sister had joined her, and she had done her best to make them comfortable even as mortar bombs continued to fall on the town. But she'd grown increasingly worried for her father's safety, since Monsieur Desbarats could not join them there — only the town's women and children took refuge in the casemates. Able-bodied civilians like Monsieur Desbarats were called upon to assist soldiers in defending the town. Although he visited his family as often as he could, his wife and daughters feared for his safety each time he left.

Before leaving Marie-Claire at the Bastion du Roi and reporting for duty, I promised her I would check on her father, something I had done at the end of my watch during each of the past three days. Although Monsieur Desbarats was clearly unaccustomed to military service, he was in good spirits and eager to support the garrison in any way he could. I conveyed his best wishes to his wife and daughters each time I visited Marie-Claire, yet the worry lines on her face deepened with each passing day. I longed to erase them, but that would only happen when the British no longer posed a threat. I looked once more toward the hillside and offered a second silent prayer that Lieutenant Colonel Marin's sortie would be able to eliminate that threat, at least for the time being.

Somewhere in the distance, a muffled cry arose from the darkness, followed by another. I could see nothing, but I knew the meaning of those cries. Marin and his men had begun their grim work.

The element of surprise appeared to work in our favour. For one hour. Shortly after that, however, musket fire shattered the air as the British grew aware of the attack and retaliated. Amid the flare of gunpowder on both sides, I could see Marin's men returning en masse from the hill, the British at their heels. The soldiers on the wall began firing over our comrades' heads to give them cover, allowing them to pour through the gate, many of them limping, while others were supported by their brothers in arms. And among them were more than two dozen prisoners.

Once all were inside and the gate closed, I offered what help I could to the wounded. One of them, Bouchard, a soldier from another company, had been shot in the leg. As I wrapped it in a makeshift bandage to halt the flow of blood, I asked him if the sortie had been successful.

"We held the hill for an hour," he explained, pain lining his face. "They were not expecting so bold a move. Our bayonets took several of their soldiers before their leaders discovered what was happening."

"Were our labourers able to destroy their entrenchments?"

"Those we reached." He winced as I tightened the bandage. "But when the alarm was raised, we were no match for their greater numbers. More than a dozen of our men were cut down before Marin ordered the retreat."

Success, it seemed, had been snatched from our grasp once again.

I worked through the night tending to wounds as best I could. When dawn arrived, I watched as men, dispatched by Governor Drucour, left the town to request a truce so that we might bury our dead, whose bodies dotted the hillside. The British granted that request and, despite numbing weariness, I volunteered to go with them. If I couldn't fight, I could at least accompany those sent to collect the fallen.

It was I who found Sergeant Fournier. His hands still gripping his musket, he lay face up, his eyes open toward the sky as if he were contemplating the shapes of clouds. It was only when my comrades lifted him into the wagon that I saw the back of his head was gone. Weeks earlier, such a sight would have left me retching. Now, all I felt was loss. And an overwhelming hopelessness.

Chapter 18
July 16, 1758

Rain battered the rampart where I stood watch, and from time to time I thought I heard thunder roll overhead. But I could not be certain, because the sound so closely resembled the boom of cannons that had continued to fire upon us since Marin's battalion had attacked the British entrenchments a week ago.

An explosion to my left nearly knocked me from my feet. Turning, I could see a huge cavity now carved in the massive west wall, a section Guillaume and I had repaired months earlier. But now all that work was for naught. Another strike would surely breach the wall and allow the enemy in.

I was grateful for the rain that had drummed Louisbourg for days because it hindered the British in their ability to target specific sites. This last strike had no doubt been the result of luck rather than keen marksmanship, and I was confident the enemy could not duplicate it easily. Of course, that same bad weather also made our defence of the town more challenging. Like the enemy, our artillerymen found it difficult to aim our guns accurately in driving rain. Worse, the rain often soaked our fuses, making it impossible to light them. And it had become a constant struggle to keep our gunpowder dry.

One thing the rain had not done was keep the British from repairing the entrenchments that Marin's labourers had destroyed. Nor had the rain stopped them from building new ones. Our artillery engineer, Grillot de Poilly, reported to Governor Drucour that he had heard sounds of men working in the darkness, and he feared the British were constructing entrenchments even closer to the town. His fears were realized the following day when the enemy began firing from new batteries nearer the wall. Only the continued rain limited the accuracy of those new British guns. But the rain would not last forever.

Our labourers worked continuously to repair the damage, and our artillerymen, both on the ramparts and on our vessels in the harbour, continued to fire upon the enemy in the hope of disrupting their advance. But the British noose was tightening even further.

My comrades talked at length about what needed to be done. All agreed that we desperately required additional support, but there still had been no word from Boishébert and his battalion, and many began to doubt they would ever arrive. With the British surrounding us, there was no way for us to determine if help would be coming from elsewhere.

It became clear last night that Governor Drucour and his war council had arrived at the same conclusion and were willing to undertake drastic measures to obtain support. Still under the command of Jean Vauquelin, the frigate *Aréthuse* hauled anchor at ten o'clock and made its way under cover of darkness toward the harbour entrance, skirting the vessels lying submerged on the channel floor. Unlike the other naval commanders who had wanted merely to escape Louisbourg to continue the fight for King Louis elsewhere, Vauquelin carried letters to the Minister of the Marine, written by Drucour and others on the war council, describing our situation. Should those letters reach their destination in time, they surely could not be ignored.

I was at my post on the rampart overlooking the harbour when *Aréthuse* began her run for the sea. As I peered into the darkness, watching her dim shape move past the quay toward the harbour entrance, I prayed she would be successful. Neither I nor the surviving members of my company truly believed it possible for us to fend off the British for the time it would take help to arrive, but what little hope remained was suddenly pinned to that single ship. My lips moved in silent prayer for its success.

Suddenly cannon fire erupted from Pointe à la Phare — the British sentries had no doubt spotted *Aréthuse* moving toward the ocean. Those of us standing watch on the rampart made the sign of the cross as the water around our frigate exploded again and again.

"Mon Dieu!" cursed a man beside me when a shot struck her stern.

I barely knew him, but I shared his apprehension. Would *Aréthuse* be lost as *Echo* had been? I made the sign of the cross and watched as our frigate continued toward the ocean. We could see her more easily now as men on her deck fought to extinguish a blaze, but this meant that the enemy could see her more easily, too.

Vauquelin was surely a skilled captain. Despite the cannon fire that followed her, he navigated *Aréthuse* smoothly among the masts and spars of the sunken ships before finally reaching open water. A cheer rose up along the rampart as she sailed off, every sentry giving voice, and the loudest of all belonged to the man beside me. *"Elle va nous sauver!"* he shouted, his eyes gleaming in the torchlight.

I, too, hoped that *Aréthuse* would save us, but she still had to run the blockade beyond the harbour. One thing in her favour, though, was her size. Smaller and faster than the warships in her path, she could manoeuvre more easily, and possibly avoid being targeted by their cannons. After suffering so many losses, surely we would be permitted this one success.

Standing on the rampart now, I could not help but wonder if that success had been achieved. I glanced again at the cavity in the wall that yawned toward the sky like the mouth of a beast demanding to be fed. And fed it would be when labourers began the task of filling it in, racing the rain-driven erosion that threatened to crumble the edges and widen the hole.

"De l'Espérance!"

Chevalier de Queue was approaching along the rampart.

"Oui, mon commandant?" I replied.

Formerly the second officer aboard the *Apollon*, the chevalier was now in charge of the Pointe à Rochefort battery, where I had served numerous times during the siege. He had an abrupt manner and he drove his men hard, but he achieved the results he desired, and it was rumoured among the garrison that he had attracted the favour of the governor. To my mind, no officer would ever command the respect of his men as Captain Boudier had done, but the chevalier seemed a fair man, never asking more of one soldier than another. And he appeared to have taken an interest in my service because of my detailed knowledge of the surrounding area. Twice during the past week he had sought me out to ask advice regarding the terrain, and I suspected that was what he wanted now. But I was wrong.

"My sergeant was killed this morning," he said as he reached me. He wiped at the water streaming down his face and cursed the rain.

"Je suis désolé," I said, but my response was mechanical. While the death of every French soldier was regrettable, Sergeant Arnaud Tremblay, a man who seemed to work far harder at shirking his duty than performing it, would not be mourned long.

The chevalier waved aside my sympathy. "I would like you to assume his duties," he said.

Surprised, I groped for words. "Surely there are others who are better suited — "

"I require a soldier who is both intelligent and skilled," he said. "You have proven to be both."

"Merci — " I began, but again he waved my words aside.

"Come with me," he ordered.

My boots sloshing, I fell into step beside him. I wanted to ask him where we were going, but his curt manner did not invite questions. It took only moments, though, for me to guess our destination— the governor's apartments.

Once there, we removed our sopping outerwear, and I accompanied him into a large room already filled with officers seated at a table — the war council who had guided the garrison's defence since the beginning of the siege. Silently cursing the coarseness of my livery, I felt my face burn as I stood tongue-tied in their presence. When the chevalier drew up a chair and sat at the table, I moved toward the wall behind him and stood in silence.

As a door opened and the governor entered, conversations around the table ceased. "It appears we are all assembled," he said, seating himself. His face drawn and grey, Drucour looked old beyond his years. "I bring good news," he said. "It would seem that *Aréthuse* has managed to elude the blockade."

All the officers around the table nodded and voiced their approval.

"One of our scouts returned an hour ago," Drucour continued. "This cursed rain allowed him to slip between enemy entrenchments and approach the Porte Dauphine unseen. He was north of Pointe à la Phare this morning and saw no sign of *Aréthuse*, nor did he see any wreckage to suggest she was destroyed. My dispatches to the Minister of the Marine are now en route."

More murmurs of approval circulated around the table, but I ignored them. Instead I focused on the governor, who did not seem as buoyed by this news as the other council members were. When he spoke again, my suspicions were confirmed.

"Unfortunately, the scout brought other news that is not so welcome." He drew a breath. "Like the rest of you here, I have anxiously awaited news of Charles Deschamps de Boishébert's arrival. Given the size of the enemy force surrounding us, I had no illusions that all twelve hundred of his men would reach Louisbourg, but even half that number would be welcome support."

The men listening murmured agreement. Six hundred men would surely strengthen our garrison, which daily lost soldiers to British artillery.

"Unfortunately," said the governor, "skirmishes with the British, combined with illness and fatigue, have taken their toll on Boishébert's men, and others have chosen to desert." He held up a piece of paper, which I assumed was a note from Boishébert. "He has barely one hundred forty men remaining, far too few to carry out the mission he was assigned." Drucour laid the paper on the table, and there was no need for him to state the obvious. Each man in the room understood perfectly the words that had gone unsaid.

Boishébert and his men would not be coming.

We were on our own.

Chapter 19
July 17, 1758

I raised my hand to Marie-Claire's face, brushing aside a lock of her hair. She looked away, no doubt mortified by her appearance, but there was no reason for her to be — the casemates offered protection, but little else. Besides, my own uniform was mottled with mud, for which I was grateful. It masked the blood and gore of comrades who had died beside me that morning.

"Mon amour," I murmured, gently taking her hand in mine, *"je t'aime."*

She smiled, but her eyes revealed a weariness that hadn't been there before. Yes, this siege was taking a heavy toll on the soldiers, but it was having the same effect on the civilians sheltered in the Bastion du Roi. These women and their children might not be dodging weapon fire on the ramparts, but they were terrified each time they heard a mortar bomb or cannonball hit, no doubt fearing for husbands or fathers or brothers or sons amid those explosions.

"I spoke to your father this morning," I told Marie-Claire now. "He is doing well." This was, at best, an exaggeration. At worst, it was a lie, since no one in Louisbourg could truthfully be described as doing well. But Monsieur Desbarats had managed a smile as I greeted him on the wall.

My words seemed to have their desired effect, and her face brightened. "When will I see him again?" she asked.

I understood the true intent of her question. Yes, she wanted to know when she might once more go to her father. But beneath her query was another that was far more crucial: When would the siege finally be over?

Developments beyond the town's walls suggested that the answer to this second question was *Soon*. At first light, Chevalier de Queue and I had walked the western ramparts to assess the enemy's movements. To our dismay, the British had dug entrenchments three hundred paces from the walls during the night.

The chevalier had immediately ordered our men to begin bombarding these new batteries, and the enemy had retaliated with weapon fire of their own, each side suffering heavy losses. It was, in fact, the blood of two of those men firing on the rampart beside me that lay hidden beneath the mud on my uniform.

I looked at Marie-Claire and answered her question the only way I knew how. "Soon," I whispered.

Chapter 20
July 21, 1758

Three more of our comrades deserted in the night, one of them Marceau, who had been in the hospital with me.

"Are you surprised?" asked Christophe when he told me.

I had seen Christophe only briefly during the month since he had saved my life. When he was not at his post, he was either in the Hôtel de la Marine or his barracks bed recovering from the effects of the rum he had swilled. Today I had nearly passed him on the rampart without recognizing him. His uniform hung on his frame like rags on a scarecrow, and in place of his ruddy complexion was a ghastly, pale hue, his scarred forehead and bloodshot eyes making him look more demonic than human.

"*Non,*" I replied, "I'm not surprised." And I wasn't. I had already heard news of the desertions. Marceau had simply joined the growing band of those who had chosen to flee Louisbourg.

While I cursed the loss of yet another comrade,

a part of me could understand Marceau's decision. There were times as I viewed the shattered landscape around us that I felt a similar desire. Two things, however, always kept me from leaving. The first was Marie-Claire, whom I could never abandon. The other was my continued desire to avenge Guillaume. Far more British soldiers would die by my hand before I was satisfied the enemy had paid the price of his death.

Christophe looked now toward the Porte Dauphine. "Do you think that's the reason for the sortie's delay?" he asked, nodding toward the two ruined batteries beyond it.

"*Je ne sais pas*," I replied, but I suspected as much. The loss of those batteries was another major blow to our defences.

He scowled. "Surely it will go ahead as planned," he said.

I shared that desire. With our situation growing ever grimmer, Governor Drucour and his war council had ordered a major offensive against the enemy today. Covered by weapon fire from our anchored ships and those two Porte Dauphine batteries, twelve hundred men were to leave the town at dawn to drive the British back from their entrenchments. It was a bold plan, and a desperate one considering the extent of our losses so far. But the council was right. We could not continue to focus all of our efforts on Louisbourg's defence. Soon we would exhaust those resources, making us completely vulnerable to an all-out attack. The only possible solution at this point was to move against the enemy.

Now under the command of the Chevalier de Queue, I was expected to follow him into battle, but I would have gone regardless of my duty. And eyeing Christophe's ragged appearance, I suspected his reasons for wishing to take part in the sortie were the same as my own. He, too, had lost people he cared for. He, too, was tired of watching the British draw closer each day. He, too, had grown weary waiting for what could only be the inevitable. Rather than perishing in a full-fledged assault that would surely come before long, he would die fighting the enemy now, and he would take as many of those British dogs with him as he could. Both of us would.

But the sortie had not yet happened.

The British had increased their weapon fire yesterday, bombarding and destroying the two batteries near the Porte Dauphine that would have provided the sortie necessary protection. Without them, the offensive would surely suffer casualties, and the loss of so many lives would be grave, especially in light of our diminishing garrison. I suspected the council was now considering this, which no doubt explained why the offensive had not yet taken place.

Besides the ruined batteries, we had sustained a second crippling loss. During their recent barrage, the British had struck a warship as well, further reducing our weaponry. Christophe gestured toward the ruined vessel, which now lay swamped in shallow water. "Such a waste," he said.

I was about to agree when an enormous explosion drowned out my words. A British mortar bomb struck *Célèbre*, which was anchored near four other warships close to the quay.

"*Mon Dieu!*" I cried as flames from the explosion already soared into the rigging. Obviously the bomb had landed on powder cartridges stored on the deck. Christophe and I watched helplessly as the fire spread, driven by the wind. Despite their dampness, both wood and sails seemed to ignite easily, and that wind carried sparks toward the sails of two other warships. Worse, the unmoored *Célèbre* was now adrift, moving perilously toward the others. In moments both *Entreprenant* and *Capricieux* were ablaze, stores of gunpowder on their decks exploding almost simultaneously.

All the men on our rampart were now staring at

the ships, some murmuring prayers for the safety of *Bienfaisant* and *Prudent*, the two remaining ships. Fortunately, *Prudent* was upwind of the fires, and the quick-thinking crew of *Bienfaisant* was able to manoeuvre the ship out of reach of the flames just in time.

Along with sparks and smoke, the wind blowing across the harbour brought with it something else — the jubilant cheers of British soldiers revelling in our loss. To them, the display must have seemed like fireworks launched in celebration of their superior might.

I turned and ran toward the waterfront with Christophe and others at my heels, intending to help in whatever way I could. A part of me expected even the British to show some sense of humanity. Surely they would reduce their bombardment in the face of so many men lost. But I was wrong. Before I could get to the quay, multiple explosions from the British cannons blocked us from reaching it.

I shouted a wordless cry that was lost in the pandemonium before us.

But there were more horrors awaiting. Many more.

Chapter 21
July 22, 1758

I lay awake in my barracks bed listening to a clock chiming the fourth hour. Despite my weariness, I had been unable to sleep as my mind recalled images of the horrors I had witnessed the day before. The worst was my memory of sailors engulfed in flames aboard all three ships, some scuttling madly in circles on the decks as they burned. As I'd approached the quay, I thought I could smell burning flesh. My stomach heaved and I vomited helplessly in the street, gagging again and again until I thought my guts would cover my boots. Even now, as I lay in the darkness, I could taste bile in my throat.

My heart blazed again with hatred for the British, who had cheered as our sailors burned to death. I wanted nothing more than to be first out of the Porte Dauphine as our troops swept over the enemy entrenchments, but the sortie was not to happen. With *Célèbre*, *Entreprenant* and *Capricieux* now destroyed, the council's plans for an assault were cancelled. The elimination of the two Porte Dauphine batteries would have made the sortie difficult, but without support from our warships, it would be impossible to overpower the enemy. There could be no thought now of risking more lives on a mission that was doomed to fail — our garrison could not sustain further losses.

I swung my feet off the bed and sat up, certain now that sleep would not come. British cannons had fired sporadically throughout the night, leaving me wondering where the next bombs might fall. So far, the sound of explosions had seemed to come from the area around the Bastion Dauphin, but I still could not suppress a sense of dread.

I stood up, my boots already on my feet, and paced the room, listening to the snores of the men who, like myself, were off duty. I envied them their ability to sleep. I had slept through mortar fire before, but this felt different somehow.

I recalled my uneasiness the day Guillaume was killed, which led me to think once more of my fallen friend. Would he mock me if he were here now? Taunt me for my restlessness? I tried to imagine his jibes, which had always lifted my spirits. But no. Guillaume would not ridicule me. In fact, I almost felt as if he were responsible for my anxiety in some way.

I shook my head at the absurdity of that thought,

but I could not ignore the feeling that something was not right and that Guillaume would have agreed with me. I moved to my bed and reached for my coat.

"Sébastien?" Christophe was looking up at me from his own bed.

"*Oui?*" I whispered.

"Is something wrong?"

I shrugged. "*Je ne sais pas.*"

"Where are you going?"

"That I don't know, either," I replied. Suddenly I feared that Christophe might think me a deserter, but I needn't have worried.

"I'll come with you," he said, pushing himself to his feet and pulling on his coat.

I nodded. Perhaps together we could determine what was bothering me. Threading through the rows of beds, we made our way toward the doorway and stepped outside.

Without warning, several explosions ripped the air, none of them from our cannons. The British were now firing upon us with an intensity we'd never seen, shots coming from both their left and right fronts. I couldn't be sure of the number of weapons discharging, because the cannon fire echoed as it rolled into the distance, but there had to be at least forty guns bombarding us. Perhaps more.

Mortar bombs screamed overhead as Christophe and I ran toward our post on the rampart. But before we reached the wall, an explosion behind us shook the ground and threw us to our knees. The barracks we'd just left had taken a direct hit. Fire already engulfed the roof and was spreading quickly.

My comrades and I ran for buckets, but there was little we could do. The water we carried to douse the fire was useless against the blaze. A handful of men burst from the barracks, rolling on the ground to smother flames licking at their clothing and their hair, but others trapped inside could only scream as the blaze overtook them. Staring helplessly at the flames that devoured friends and the only home I had known for two years, I felt as if I were peering into the fiery pit of hell. Nothing could be worse.

But I was wrong. Explosions ripped the air to the east of us as several of the bombs targeting the Bastions du Roi, de la Reine and Dauphin overshot their marks and landed in the centre of town, setting civilian buildings ablaze. I felt my heart stagger as a new Hades erupted behind us.

Mercifully, the screams inside the barracks had ceased. I could do nothing more for our comrades there, nor could the structure be saved, so

I ran toward this new horror, other soldiers right behind me. The homes and businesses that had been struck were already fully engulfed.

My feet pounded over the cobblestones past townsmen struggling to keep the fire from spreading, but I ignored them as I raced toward Rue de l'Étang. Marie-Claire would want news of her father, who had remained in their home, and I prayed the street had escaped mortar fire.

My prayers went unanswered. Two of the homes on Rue de l'Étang had taken direct hits, one of them belonging to Monsieur Desbarats. The explosion was so powerful, the heat so intense, that I felt it even as I turned onto the street. Although there could be no survivors, I forced my feet to carry me closer. I now prayed that I was mistaken, that the flickering shadows cast by the blaze had confused me and the Desbarats' home still stood. But the toe of my boot kicked something hard. It was an iron ring with the letter *D* at its centre, the very knocker I had rapped the evening I asked for Marie-Claire's hand in marriage. Fifty-two days and several lifetimes ago.

Whatever false hope I clung to vanished. I stood there in the street staring at that iron ring, knowing I must tell Marie-Claire of her father's death, yet searching for the strength merely to remain standing.

At some point I was able to shrug off my shock

and make my way toward the casemates, often backtracking to avoid debris and craters in the streets. And despite the urgency of my mission, I slowed as I neared my destination, dreading the task before me. But there was no need for me to say the words. Marie-Claire could read them on my face the moment my eyes found hers.

Holding her tightly as she sobbed, I silently raged at the enemy, fearing that the news I had just delivered would break her. Marie-Claire had been so strong throughout the siege, but a person's strength is not limitless. Had she not already borne for weeks the threat of death at the hands of the enemy? Had she not been forced to leave her comfortable home and live in the cold, cramped casemates? Had she not helped support me as I reeled from the loss of Guillaume? Had she not coped with the sight of me lying wounded in the hospital, then spent days nursing me back to health? How could her father's death not shatter her?

The only consolation I could possibly offer Marie-Claire was that he had surely died the instant the bomb struck. He hadn't lain broken and trapped beneath burning rubble, writhing in agony. But this I did not share with her. I could not. There was nothing anyone could say that would make her loss less painful.

Sounds of cannon fire and mortar explosions continued to pierce the air, yet still I held her. Finally, after several shuddering moments, she pulled away and wiped at her tears. "I must go to them," she said, nodding toward her mother and sister, who clung to each other as though drowning. Their wails made the walls ring.

I watched, stunned, as Marie-Claire moved toward them, kneeling at their side and whispering gently, her words of no real consequence. In the face of her own anguish, she was still able to offer her compassion and her strength. Both made me love her even more.

But I could watch no longer — there was much that needed to be done. Despite the futility of our efforts, I would continue to fight. Not because I served at the pleasure of King Louis, but to defend the woman I loved.

I could do nothing less.

*   *   *

Nearly a hundred people, both soldiers and civilians, had perished in the attack. Fire had taken lives as surely as mortar bombs and musket shot. And more continued to perish as the British began bombarding Louisbourg, bombs crashing into both military and civilian buildings.

Fear gripped the town, and more and more men

had begun slipping over the wall, preferring to live as traitors than die as soldiers. Officers throughout the garrison were losing men, and the Chevalier de Queue repeatedly bemoaned the growing problem. "I shudder to think what information those cowards are giving the enemy," he snarled now as he lit the fuse on the twenty-four-pounder I had just reloaded.

I didn't respond. What information could those men possibly provide that the British didn't already possess? Hadn't I just loaded scrap metal into the barrel of this cannon? When hinges and hammerheads began raining down upon the heads of our enemies, would they not realize we had exhausted most of our ammunition? What more was there to know?

I suddenly thought of my poor father in France, of the chickens he would butcher those rare times when there was money to buy them. He would lay them across a wooden block and cut off their heads with a single swipe of his axe. They died instantly, yet for long moments afterwards their headless bodies would continue to flap their wings and run around the yard, colliding with anything in their path.

Louisbourg was like those chickens. She was already dead but had not yet realized it.

Chapter 22
July 25, 1758

His pale face smudged with soot and gunpowder, Christophe turned to me. "There's nothing else," he said, pointing to where we had piled scrap metal scavenged from the town. Our last shot had sent iron from a broken pair of tongs hurtling toward the enemy and, for a brief moment, I almost laughed. I wondered about the chances of that iron striking a British soldier who, in his former civilian life, might have been a blacksmith. Such odd thoughts were commonplace now. Since the British had begun their continuous assault, no one had been able to rest, and I was beyond exhausted, both in body and in spirit.

Of course, we had no idea if our shots were striking the enemy. In fact, we had no idea if they were striking anywhere close to them. Thick fog had blanketed the area all day and, as the hour now approached midnight, darkness was an equally impenetrable cloak. The chevalier had given up checking the cannon's aim. Each time I sponged and primed the cannon, he simply lit the fuse with a shrug. At this point, all we could do was return fire and pray our shots hit their mark. Because of the enemy's far greater numbers and their positions so close to the town, at least some of our volleys would do their work.

But now, without ammunition, aim was the least of our concerns.

During the past twenty-four hours, I had left my post only three times, twice to collect scrap metal and once more to help fight fires. The Bastion de la Reine had received a direct hit that ignited a major blaze, which the wind fanned and spread to two nearby buildings. All three quickly became an inferno, which I was certain would spread through the entire town. Thankfully, Providence shone on us — the wind changed direction, allowing the fire to be contained.

That, however, was our only good fortune. The wall had been breached in at least two places, yet still the enemy pummelled us with mortar bombs and cannonballs. More soldiers had deserted since the latest bombardment began, and increasing numbers had been wounded or killed. We could not hope to hold off the British much longer. More than anything, I longed to go to Marie-Claire, but with our situation so desperate, there was no time. I was grateful that the guns of *Prudent* and

Bienfaisant continued to fire upon the enemy, but I wondered when they, too, would run short of ammunition.

"De l'Espérance."

I turned toward the chevalier, my ears still ringing from the last firing of the cannon. *"Oui?"*

He nodded toward Christophe. "Take Gilbert and scour the town for more metal."

I knew there was little nearby that would fit inside the barrel of the cannon. Like us, other soldiers had been scavenging for metal, going from building to building and taking whatever they could carry. "We will have to go farther into the town," I said.

"Allez!" he commanded, then moved off along the rampart to assess the growing damage.

Christophe and I each took a handle of a large, two-wheeled cart we'd used twice before and eased it from the rampart down the slope toward the parade square. The earth was now heavily cratered and strewn with rubble, which made even walking difficult, so pulling an empty cart was a trial. Pulling that same cart back carrying scrap metal would be much worse.

"Should we try Rue d'Estrées?" Christophe asked.

I nodded. Others probably wouldn't have taken

the time to go as far as the street beyond the hospital, so surely there would be scrap metal among the buildings there. I guided us past the parade square toward Rue de France. I had no wish to follow Rue d'Orléans, which would have taken us past the remains of Marie-Claire's house.

Enemy fire continued to shatter the air, repeatedly striking the wall and making the ground beneath our feet shake. Screams somewhere behind us rose from the darkness, and then halted abruptly as another explosion shook the earth. Suddenly the whistle of an approaching mortar bomb pierced the air, and Christophe and I dove beneath the cart. The bomb struck less than thirty paces to our left, smashing the ground like Thor's hammer and throwing cobblestones and earth into the air, a wave of rocky spray covering the floor of the cart above our heads.

Even in the darkness, I caught the gleam in Christophe's eyes, the same bizarre anticipation that all of us had begun to feel. Most of the garrison at this point was beyond fear. Not that we didn't experience it — we'd merely grown numb to its effects. And how could we not? After weeks of constant anxiety and dread, weeks of seeing our comrades writhing in pain and dying in our arms, each of us expected that every moment, every breath, would be our last. In some strange way, that expectation had become a gift, the only thing that made many of us capable of enduring the horror that each day had become — the knowledge that it would soon all be over. After the hell we had endured for so long, death could only be a blessing.

Our ears still ringing, Christophe and I waited beneath the cart a moment longer to see if the British would continue targeting our area, and I suddenly found myself grinning at the absurdity of our supposed safety. The cart could offer no protection whatsoever from the bombs. Christophe grinned sheepishly in return, and the two of us crawled out from under it, pulled ourselves to our feet and continued on our way.

We had gotten no farther than Rue Dauphine when we heard drummers beating the *générale*, signalling an immediate call to arms. Scant moments later, several men ran past us down the hill toward the harbour crying, *"Aux armes! Aux armes!"* Without speaking, Christophe and I dropped the handles of the cart and raced toward the waterfront, our progress hindered by deep holes and debris everywhere.

We saw it long before we reached the quay.

"Sébastien!" moaned Christophe beside me, his voice hollow. *Prudent* was in flames.

"How — ?" Christophe began again, but there was no need for him to finish his thought.

The same question burned across my own mind. How could this have happened? Had not the loss of *Célèbre*, *Entreprenant* and *Capricieux* shown our officers the need to protect our remaining warships? Surely *Prudent* had been anchored far enough beyond the range of British guns to avoid being struck by cannon fire. And no British ships had ventured into the harbour to fire upon her. Only the outline of *Bienfaisant* could be seen nearby.

I peered through the swirling fog toward *Prudent,* now illuminated by the soaring flames. Several longboats floated beside her, each filled with British sailors. How could they possibly have rowed into the harbour and taken the ship without being detected?

But the answer was simple. The fog had offered them the cover they needed, and their land forces had kept our attention focused on the western approach to the town, providing exactly the distraction they required to execute such a daring move beneath our very noses.

Yet why had *Bienfaisant* not given aid? Her crew would have seen the assault, would they not? And why weren't they firing upon the enemy even now? Once more, I peered through the fog, trying to understand.

"*Mon Dieu!*" Christophe exclaimed, just as my eyes found what I had missed before in the fog. British colours now flew above *Bienfaisant*.

Curses and cries of frustration rose along the waterfront as the men who'd reached the harbour before us arrived at the same realization. Each drew his musket and began firing upon the vessel. Christophe joined them, his oaths mingling with theirs, but the enemy aboard *Bienfaisant* persevered. They had cut the anchor lines, and already the ship was moving into deeper water. *Bienfaisant* now belonged to the British.

I did not lift my own musket to fire upon her. There was no point.

Our naval support was gone, the harbour now defenceless. At first light, any number of British warships would sail unhindered into the anchorage and aim their guns on the town. The noose had at last been cinched tight. The siege was over.

Bloody and headless, the creature that was Louisbourg now had no choice but to acknowledge its own death.

Epilogue

July 26, 1758
9:47 a.m.

As Major Loppinot and I continue along what remains of Rue Toulouse, a sudden breeze off the water catches the flag I carry, making the heavy cotton flutter and snap above my head. For some reason, this unexpected movement lifts my heart. There has been so much death within these walls, and so much more yet to come, that even the semblance of life in the flag seems heaven-sent.

We reach the quay and turn left to follow the water. I try to keep my eyes forward, try to keep them from scanning the many warships now anchored at the mouth of the harbour. Aboard one of those ships is a mortar bomb that will no doubt end my life, but I care not. I will die in the service of my king because that is my lot, the end of the path I chose in join-ing the Compagnies Franches de la Marine. What rends my heart now is that somewhere aboard one of those vessels is the gun that will target the Bastion du Roi and bring its casemate stones crashing down, crushing the life from the woman I love. My fervent prayers that Marie-Claire might somehow be spared have gone unanswered. I yearn to see her face once more, but the only faces before me now are those of the battle-weary soldiers who have shared with me the horror and the futility of these past weeks.

We approach the ruin that is the Porte Dauphine. Beyond it lies the makeshift encampment where Major Loppinot will meet Major General Amherst and Admiral Boscawen a final time. Britain's cursed Great Union flag hoisted above it seems to mock us, its crosses of Saint George and Saint Andrew further proclaiming our enemy's victory and our loss.

I wonder how Amherst and Boscawen will respond to Governor Drucour's refusal to submit to their unreasonable demands. Will they show surprise? Disappointment? Anger? None of this matters, of course, but these idle thoughts keep my mind from returning to Marie-Claire and the life we will never have together.

I wonder if I will be permitted a final opportunity to see her. Will those British warships begin to make their way into the harbour today to let loose their barrage, or will the enemy wait until tomorrow, giving families and loved ones time to say goodbye before the guns begin to fire? I long

*for that chance, but is this fair to Marie-Claire?
As strong as she has proven herself to be, can she
withstand one more night with the knowledge that
certain death awaits her? Am I so selfish that
I would want her to endure that? I consider this
question, turning my answers over in my head as
each step takes us closer to our doom.*

"Major Loppinot! Wait!"

*Both the major and I turn to see the Chevalier
de Courserac, the former captain of the* Bienfaisant,
*hurrying toward us. His face is red and he gasps
for breath. When he finally reaches us, he bends
over and places his hands on his knees, panting.
"Merci," he says at last. "I have important news
from Drucour."*

"Quelles sont les nouvelles?" *asks Loppinot.*

*Catching his breath, the chevalier says the one
thing that I have fervently prayed for since realizing
our defeat was unavoidable. "We are to surrender."*

*Major Loppinot seems as relieved as I, but still he
asks the question: "On the enemy's terms?"*

*The chevalier nods. "The war council has accepted
all of them."*

*I listen dumbfounded as the chevalier explains
that it is Jacques Prévost, the town's financial
administrator, to whom we owe this change of
heart. As expected, he had argued for the lives*

of Louisbourg's civilians, but it was the economic value those lives represented that held sway in the minds of the war council members. If our civilians were slaughtered, said Prévost, the world might think that King Louis was unable to protect his citizens. And if King Louis lost the confidence of the merchants he relied on to help him broaden his holdings, no financier in the future would agree to sponsor another venture.

The reason for the war council's change of heart is of no consequence to me. What matters is that my prayers have been answered after all. Marie-Claire will live, and the British will return her and her family to France. I and my comrades, of course, will be taken to Britain and held as prisoners of war, but even this does not trouble me. God has answered my prayers that Marie-Claire be spared, and I know He will answer my prayers to be reunited with her. At some point, I, too, will be released and returned to France. This war will not last forever. It cannot. With Louisbourg now fallen, there is nothing to keep the British from invading the rest of New France. These past few weeks were the beginning of the end of French rule in the New World. I am certain of it.

Another breeze off the harbour lifts and ripples the flag I carry, making it snap overhead, and I am suddenly filled with an emotion that, at first, I do not recognize. It seems foreign to me because it has been so long since I have felt it.

Hope.

Historical Note

The Seven Years War, which officially began in 1756 and continued until 1763, was the first global conflict because it involved multiple countries: Great Britain and the German states of Prussia and Hanover were allied against France, Austria, Sweden, Russia and the German state of Saxony. In North America, the Seven Years War involved only two of those nations, Great Britain and France, as each tried to enforce its claim to the continent. The siege of Louisbourg in 1758 was a significant chapter in that struggle because France's loss of its Île Royale (Cape Breton Island) fortification weakened the country's ability to protect its holdings in New France. Even more important than its defence of the entrance to the Gulf of St. Lawrence was the fact that Louisbourg was a key fishing base and export centre for the cod fishery. Besides being invaluable to French merchants, the fishery also provided France with a pool of experienced sailors who could be called into naval service if needed. The French would never recover from Louisbourg's loss, which signalled the beginning of the end of French control in North America.

Throughout history, the primary force that has driven countries to expand their domination of new lands is commerce. Nations longed to increase their wealth by acquiring new sources of goods that they could trade. When explorer Giovanni Caboto, better known as John Cabot, first sailed to the New World in 1497 and returned with reports of rich fishing grounds off its coast, several countries took action to colonize the region. England, France and Scotland were among them.

In 1713 the French settled at Louisbourg on Île Royale, a location that provided a fine harbour from which men could fish the nearby waters for cod. Plans were developed in 1717 for a fortified town, and in 1719 King Louis XV ordered the construction of Louisbourg to begin. It would have three functions: as a fortress, it would guard the entrance to the Gulf of St. Lawrence, helping protect New France from enemy invasion; as a seaport, it would offer excellent anchorage for ships that brought much-needed supplies and left with their cargo holds filled with salted cod; finally, it would provide a community for its citizens — both military and civilian — who came from a variety of countries and cultural backgrounds.

The construction of the fortifications took twenty-eight years to complete, making Louisbourg one of the largest and most impressive fortresses in North America. It was also one of the most expensive, costing King Louis XV more than seven times the original budget.

The fortifications surrounding Louisbourg were, without question, an imposing sight. A wall 4 kilometres long surrounded the entire town, its seaward side nearly 5 metres high and nearly 2 metres across. Its western wall, however, was close to 10 metres high and nearly 11 metres across, its additional size and strength necessary because of the geography of the area — Louisbourg was overlooked by higher ground to the west, so increased protection from enemy attack was needed on that flank. One hundred cannons were mounted in embrasures along the wall, but these were not the only guns protecting the town. A small island in the harbour was fortified with walls 3 metres high and nearly 2.5 metres across. Thirty-one cannons defended the harbour from that position.

Each year between the 1720s and 1750s, France allotted part of its budget to developing and defending Louisbourg because Île Royale's fishery was so valuable. By the 1740s, up to seven hundred soldiers served at Louisbourg, and when the British made landfall on June 8, 1758, that number had grown to 3520 soldiers along with 2606 naval officers and sailors, making a total force of 6126 men. It is unknown exactly how many civilians made Louisbourg their home during that period, but historians believe that close to three thousand men, women and children lived within its walls.

Because of the cod fishery, Louisbourg experienced remarkable growth, and its harbour became one of the busiest in North America. Unfortunately, not all was ideal. Its citizens were not able to provide everything they required to survive. The poor soil and cool, damp climate on Cape Breton's eastern coast made agriculture difficult, so they had to import much of their food. This lack of independence would become a serious disadvantage if the town were under siege for an extended period.

Long before King Louis XV's impressive fortifications rose along the harbour, the British predicted that Louisbourg would pose a threat to them. When the fortifications were completed, those predictions became fact. As a result, in 1745 the British supported New England in an attack on the town that went on for weeks, eventually defeating the French and expelling them.

However, when England and France signed the Treaty of Aix-la-Chapelle in 1748, ending the War of the Austrian Succession, France regained control of Louisbourg, and its military and citizens returned once more to the fortified town.

Of course, Louisbourg remained the threat it had been before, which ultimately led the British to attack it again. Besides Major General Jeffery Amherst and Admiral Edward Boscawen, another notable British officer involved in the 1758 siege was Brigade Commander James Wolfe, who, a year later, led the force that captured Quebec City.

When the British set their ships to take Louisbourg in 1758, approximately twenty-eight thousand British soldiers and sailors attacked. In the face of such overwhelming numbers, the French had no hope of victory. Other factors also doomed them to failure. Because they had to import much of what they required to survive, a British blockade of Louisbourg's harbour prevented them from receiving the provisions they needed to continue their defence. And while Louisbourg's fortifications were impressive, they were best suited to repelling an attack from the sea. However, poor leadership on the part of some of the French officers enabled the British to come ashore at Anse de la Cormorandière, and the rest, as they say, is history. By July 27, 1758, the day after their surrender, 3847 French soldiers and sailors remained fit for duty at Louisbourg. They had lost 2279 brothers in arms to injury, death or desertion.

A sad truth about colonialism is that leaders in faraway countries rarely spent time thinking about the people who made those colonies their home. Monarchs were far more likely to consider economic returns than human lives when they made decisions affecting the regions they controlled. It is interesting to note that, when Louisbourg's leaders rejected the terms the British offered them for their surrender, they were willing to condemn every man, woman and child in the fortress to possible death for the sake of honour. It was only when the town's financial administrator, Jacques Prévost, put that loss in economic terms that they reconsidered. Prévost pointed out that King Louis XV would surely find it difficult — if not impossible — to attract financiers to invest in future enterprises if he could not ensure the safety of the civilians who would be a part of those enterprises. Commerce, apparently, will always be king.

After surrendering, Louisbourg's surviving soldiers and sailors were sent to England as prisoners of war. In addition, French troops on Île

Saint-Jean (present-day Prince Edward Island) were also required to surrender as prisoners of war. Civilians who did not bear arms against the British were sent to France.

After capturing Louisbourg and expelling the French a second time, the British were unwilling to see the fortification return to their enemy's hands, as had happened in the past. Therefore, British engineers systematically destroyed the town's defences so they could never be used again.

Although the fortification functioned as a French base on Cape Breton Island for a relatively short period, it played an extremely important role in the defence and development of the area. Its loss following the siege of 1758 was a major turning point in North American history. Recognizing the strong historical significance of the fortress, the Government of Canada designated Louisbourg a National Historic Site in 1928 and, in 1961, began a faithful reconstruction of one-quarter of the fortified town. This popular attraction now allows visitors to experience what it would have been like to live and work in an eighteenth-century French colonial settlement.

There were over a thousand members of the Compagnies Franches de la Marine in Louisbourg by 1758. An officer is pictured at the right, a soldier at the left.

Brigade Commander James Wolfe wades ashore through the surf at Louisbourg as the British make landfall.

Louisbourg is besieged by British ships, 1758.

One of the cannons at Fortress Louisbourg overlooks the waterfront along the quay wall. The fortress is now a National Historic Site.

The Prudent burns as Bienfaisant is captured. The loss of the ships was a major blow to Louisbourg's defenders.

In this woodcut illustration, French forces at Louisbourg surrender to the British (marching in with the Great Union flag) under the command of Major General Jeffery Amherst and Admiral Edward Boscawen.

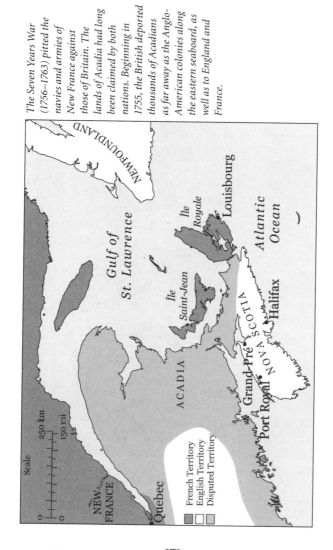

The Seven Years War (1756–1763) pitted the navies and armies of New France against those of Britain. The lands of Acadia had long been claimed by both nations. Beginning in 1755, the British deported thousands of Acadians as far away as the Anglo-American colonies along the eastern seaboard, as well as to England and France.

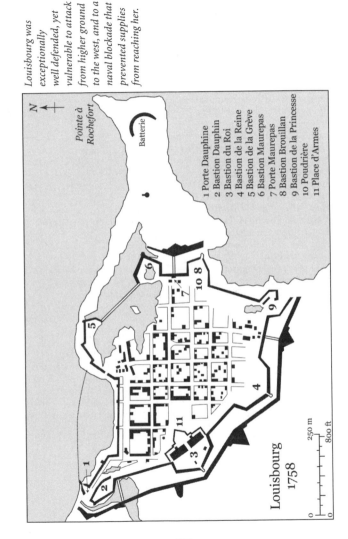

Louisbourg was exceptionally well defended, yet vulnerable to attack from higher ground to the west, and to a naval blockade that prevented supplies from reaching her.

N

Pointe à Rochefort

Batterie

1 Porte Dauphine
2 Bastion Dauphin
3 Bastion du Roi
4 Bastion de la Reine
5 Bastion de la Grève
6 Bastion Maurepas
7 Porte Maurepas
8 Bastion Brouillan
9 Bastion de la Princesse
10 Poudrière
11 Place d'Armes

Louisbourg
1758

250 m

800 ft

Credits

Cover cameo (detail): *Portrait of William Locke aged seventeen*, c.1783/4 (oil on canvas), John Hoppner, Private Collection © Philip Mould Ltd., London; Bridgeman Images, MOU289019.

Cover scene: *Capture of "The Prudent" and "Bienfaisant" in Louisbourg Harbour, 26th July 1758*, Copyright © Royal Ontario Museum, 956.94, ROM2004_1409_1.

Journal Details: supertramp88 Shutterstock, Inc.; belly band © ranplett/ istockphoto; back cover label © Thomas Bethge/Shutterstock, Inc.

Page 165: (left) *Soldier of the Compagnies Franches de la Marine of Canada, 1757–1760*; (right) *Officer of the Compagnies Franches de la Marine of Canada, circa 1750*; reconstructions by Eugène Lelièpvre, Parks Canada.

Page 166: *Wolfe wading ashore through the surf at Louisbourg*, Charles Jefferys, Library and Archives Canada, MIKAN 2835894.

Page 167: *A View of Louisbourg in North America...besieged in 1758*, Library and Archives Canada, Acc. No. R9266-818, Peter Winkworth Collection of Canadiana, MIKAN 3020573.

Page 168: *Cannon along quay at Fortress Louisbourg*; Dan Roitner/ Alamy Images.

Page 169: *The Burning of the* Prudent *and the Taking of the* Bienfaisant *in Louisbourg (Nova Scotia) Harbour, 1758*, Pierre Charles Canot, courtesy of Toronto Public Library, Baldwin Collection.

Page 170: *Surrender of Louisbourg to the British under General Jeffery Amherst, French and Indian War*, North Wind Picture Archive/Alamy Images.

Pages 171 and 172: Maps by Paul Heersink/Paperglyphs.

The publisher wishes to thank Janice Weaver for her detailed checking of the facts; and A.J.B. Johnston, a longtime historian with Parks Canada and author of the highly regarded *Endgame 1758: The Promise, the Glory, and the Despair of Louisbourg's Last Decade* and of *Grand Pré, Landscape for the World*, for his invaluable input on the manuscript.

Author's Note

I have lived my entire life in Nova Scotia, a province rich in many cultures, and I have always been interested in stories of the early French settlers. No doubt much of this interest arose from my living a short drive from Port Royal, which is considered the oldest French settlement in all of North America. When I was deciding on a focus for this novel, I immediately knew I would choose an event from French history in Atlantic Canada. The fall of Louisbourg seemed a likely subject because the loss of that fortress marked the beginning of the end for New France.

While *Brothers in Arms: The Siege of Louisbourg* is a novel, the events it describes in 1758 are historical. Sébastien de l'Espérance is fictional and I invented his name. Interestingly, however, after completing the first draft of the novel, I learned that a thirty-three-year-old man named Charles-Gabriel-Sébastien de l'Espérance lived at Louisbourg in 1758, a coincidence I found more than a little surprising. Other fictional characters in the story are Sébastien's comrades Guillaume, Jacques,

Christophe, Édouard, Renard and Marceau; military figures Captain Boudier, Corporal Grimaud, Sergeant Fournier and Sergeant Tremblay; Sébastien's fiancée, Marie-Claire; and the members of her family. However, every other person included in the novel lived in Louisbourg during the British invasion. I have depicted their roles as accurately as I could.

I have visited the Parks Canada Fortress of Louisbourg National Historic Site many times, and it was very helpful to return there while I was planning this novel. Moving through its streets and buildings gives visitors an excellent sense of what it was like to live in Louisbourg during that period. Staff members dress in period costumes and perform many of the duties that would have been required of its military and citizens at the time. Animals similar to the livestock raised by those citizens are found within the fortress walls. Garden plots produce some of the herbs and vegetables that would have been grown there, and eating establishments serve food that typically would have been eaten by the people who called Louisbourg their home. In a very real sense, it is a living museum that offers visitors an opportunity to experience eighteenth-century life in one of the most remarkable settings in North America.

During my research for this novel, I read a number of excellent books written about the rise and fall of Louisbourg. The most helpful of all was *Endgame 1758: The Promise, the Glory, and the Despair of Louisbourg's Last Decade*, written by A.J.B. Johnston. Besides being a historian and leading expert in his knowledge of the fortress and the military and citizenry who occupied it, Mr. Johnston is also a novelist whose fiction focuses on that same time period. His detailed account of the siege and ultimate surrender described in *Endgame 1758* provided much of the framework upon which I constructed the narrative of *Brothers in Arms*. In addition, he graciously responded to many questions regarding details I needed to ensure that my story accurately portrayed Louisbourg and its fall, details that not only involved the scope and sequence of events, but also elements of language.

For example, while the site is now commonly referred to as Fortress Louisbourg, Mr. Johnston pointed out that the term "fortress" was not used to describe Louisbourg until the twentieth century, which is why I have not used it in the novel itself. He also advised me on the proper spellings of *Bastion Dauphin* and *Porte Dauphine*, and concurred regarding use of the historical spelling,

Micmac, rather than the contemporary spelling, *Mi'kmaq*.

Of all the details I learned while researching the siege, the one that resonated most strongly with me was the willingness of Louisbourg's leaders to sacrifice every man, woman and child in the town when the governor's war council initially refused to accept the terms of surrender the British had given them. Their determination to fight to the death rather than suffer indignity says so much about the value the French placed on honour. When I learned about the war council's last-minute change of heart, I thought the events around that moment held the same sense of heightened drama we see so often in contemporary edge-of-your-seat thrillers. The difference, of course, was that this was real life, and these were real people whose lives hung in the balance and were spared only at the last moment. Long before I began writing my first draft, I knew immediately that I wanted to build my entire story around this scene. This is why *Brothers in Arms: The Siege of Louisbourg* not only begins and ends with it, but also pauses midway to return to Jean-Chrysostome Loppinot as he carries the single-sentence response from Governor Drucour that dooms every person within Louisbourg's walls. No author, whether writing fiction or fact, could ignore the extraordinary dramatic tension of that experience.

* * *

A former high school teacher and university instructor from Nova Scotia, Don Aker has written twenty books, among them several novels for teenagers. His young adult fiction has earned him numerous awards, including the Ontario Library Association's White Pine Award for *The First Stone*, Atlantic Canada's Ann Connor Brimer Award for *The First Stone* and *Of Things Not Seen*, the Canadian Authors Association's Lilla Stirling Award for *Of Things Not Seen* and *One on One*, and an Honour Book citation from the Canadian Library Association for *The Space Between*.

Other books in the
I AM CANADA series

Behind Enemy Lines
World War II
Carol Matas

Blood and Iron
Building the Railway
Paul Yee

A Call to Battle
The War of 1812
Gillian Chan

Deadly Voyage
RMS Titanic
Hugh Brewster

Defend or Die
The Siege of Hong Kong
Gillian Chan

Fire in the Sky
World War I
David Ward

Graves of Ice
The Lost Franklin Expedition
John Wilson

Prisoner of Dieppe
World War II
Hugh Brewster

Shot at Dawn
World War I
John Wilson

Sink and Destroy
The Battle of the Atlantic
Edward Kay

Storm the Fortress
The Siege of Quebec
Maxine Trottier

For more information please see the I AM CANADA
website: www.scholastic.ca/iamcanada